Charade

Charade

From the Classic 1963 Film

Based on a screenplay by
Peter Stone and **Marc Behm**

Published 2026 by Maple Spring Publishing

CHARADE. Copyright © 2026 Maple Spring Publishing. All rights reserved.

No part of this book may be used, reproduced or transmitted in any manner whatsoever, by any means (electronic, photocopying, recording, or otherwise), without the prior written permission of the author, except in the case of brief quotations embodied in critical articles and reviews. No liability is assumed with respect to the use of the information contained within. Although every precaution has been taken, the author and publisher assume no liability for errors or omissions. Neither is any liability assumed for damages resulting from the use of the information contained herein.

Book design by Jason Snyder

Library of Congress Cataloging-in-Publication Data is available upon request

ISBN: 979-8-3505-0225-1

10 9 8 7 6 5 4 3 2 1

Charade

Produced and Directed by **Stanley Donen**
Screenplay by **Peter Stone** and **Marc Behm**

CAST

Cary Grant as Brian Cruikshank
(alias Peter Joshua, Alexander Dyle and Adam Canfield)

Audrey Hepburn as Regina "Reggie" Lampert

Walter Matthau as Carson Dyle
(alias Hamilton Bartholomew)

James Coburn as Tex Panthollow

George Kennedy as Herman Scobie

Dominique Minot as Sylvie Gaudel

Ned Glass as Leopold W. Gideon

Jacques Marin as Inspector Edouard Grandpierre

Paul Bonifas as Mr. Felix, the stamp dealer

Thomas Chelimsky as Jean-Louis Gaudel

DISTRIBUTED BY UNIVERSAL PICTURES
RELEASE DATE 1963

FADE IN (BEFORE TITLES)

EXT. FRENCH COUNTRYSIDE—DUSK

Camera pans the green, squared-off flatland, lit only by a fine sunset in its final throes. Then, gradually, starting from nothing, a rumble is heard, quickly growing louder and louder until the sound of a train can be recognized.

Camera pans quickly, discovering the railroad line atop a man-made rise of land, and the speeding passenger train is upon us, flashing by with a roar.

Then, as if from nowhere, the figure of a man hits the embankment and rolls crazily down to the bottom into the thick underbrush alongside the tracks.

Close shot—a body lies in the bushes, still, unmoving—dead. Camera pans away to the quiet peaceful countryside as the sound of the train fades off until there is silence once more.

EXT. MEGEVE—DAY

A handsome and elegant hotel perched on the mountain-side overlooking the French resort town. A large, open sun deck—tables, gaily colored parasols, sun bathers.

One of the latter is Regina "Reggie" Lampert, a lovely young girl. She is, besides taking in the sun, involved in her favorite activity—eating. Then—a dark, ominous shape intrudes in the f.g. Focus changes to bring into sharp relief a revolver—shining, black and ugly in the

sunlight. Reggie, unaware of her danger, continues to eat. The finger tightens around the trigger and finally the gun shoots—a stream of water arcs, with unerring aim, straight into Reggie's face.

Another angle including Jean-Louis, a French boy of six or so. Reggie looks at him sternly.

JEAN-LOUIS

Oh, la.

REGGIE

Don't tell me you didn't know it was loaded.

(calling)

Sylvie!

Wider angle shows Sylvie Gaudet, French, attractive, blonde, in her early thirties, comes from the railing of the sun deck to join Reggie and Jean-Louis.

SYLVIE

Oh.

REGGIE

Can't he do something constructive? Like start an avalanche or something?

Jean-Louis scampers off. Sylvie notices Reggie's lunch which consists of cold chicken, potato salad, rolls and butter, wine and coffee.

SYLVIE

When you start to eat like this, something is the matter.

REGGIE

Sylvie, I'm getting a divorce.

SYLVIE

What? From Charles?

REGGIE

He's the only husband I have. I've tried to make it work. Really, I have.

SYLVIE

But what?

REGGIE

Oh, I can't explain. It's just that I'm too miserable to go on any longer like this.

Reggie picks up a chicken leg and starts off. Sylvie regards the devastated table before following.

SYLVIE

It is infuriating that your unhappiness does not turn to fat.

INT. SWIMMING POOL—DAY

A magnificent indoor, glass-enclosed pool, the vista of snow covered mountains seen through the ceiling-high windows beyond. Reggie and Sylvie are passing through, their conversation continuing.

SYLVIE

But I don't understand. Why do you want a divorce?

REGGIE

Because I don't love him, and he obviously doesn't love me.

SYLVIE

That's no reason to get a divorce.

EXT. HOTEL TERRACE—DAY

An open balcony running around two sides of the pool, sun-worshippers lying in deck-chairs. Reggie and Sylvie appear, their conversation continuing.

SYLVIE

With a rich husband and this year is closed, you won't find it difficult to make some new friends.

REGGIE

Look, admit I came to Paris to escape American provincial, but that doesn't mean I'm ready for French traditional. I loathe the whole idea of divorce, Sylvie, but if only Charles had been honest with me, that's all I ask of anybody; the simple truth, but with Charles, everything is secrecy and lies. He's hiding something from me, Sylvie, something terrible, and it frightens me.

She stops as she is aware of a weird figure hovering over her. She wheels, terrified.

CLOSE SHOT—PERUVIAN SNOW MASK

A strange, grotesque knitted mask that completely covers the face except for eyes, nose and mouth. The eyes inside this particular mask stare down at Reggie.

MAN

Does he belong to you?

Camera pans down to include Jean-Louis, his hand held firmly by the man in the mask.

Wider angle including Reggie, Man, Sylvie and Jean-Louis. Reggie is too terrified to answer. Realizing this, the man, Peter Joshua, takes off the snow-mask to reveal a handsome, tanned face.

REGGIE

(indicating Sylvie)

It's hers. Where'd you find him? Robbing a bank?

PETER

He was throwing snowballs at Baron Rothschild.

SYLVIE

Oh, thank you.

PETER

Do we know each other?

REGGIE

Why do you think we're going to?

PETER

I don't know. How would I know?

REGGIE

Because I already know an awful lot of people until one of them dies. I couldn't possibly meet anyone else.

PETER

Hmm. Well, if anyone goes on the critical list, let me know.

(he starts off)

REGGIE

Quitter.

PETER

Uh uhh.

REGGIE

You give up awful easily, don't you?

Eyeing one, then the other, Sylvie sizes up the situation and rises.

SYLVIE

Oui, Jean-Louis, let us take a walk. I've never seen a Rothschild before.

Sylvie and Jean-Louis start off, but not before the boy squirts Peter with his pistol.

PETER

(drying)

Clever fella. Almost miss me. Thank you.

REGGIE

You're blocking my view.

PETER

(moving)

Oh, oh, which view would you prefer?

REGGIE

The one you're blocking. It's my last chance. I'm flying back to Paris this afternoon. What's your name?

PETER

Peter Joshua.

REGGIE

Oh, mine's Reggie Lampert.

PETER

Is there a Mr. Lampert?

REGGIE

Yes.

PETER

Good for you.

REGGIE

No it isn't. I'm getting a divorce.

PETER

Please not on my account.

REGGIE

Oh no. I certain don't really love him.

PETER

Well, at least you're honest.

REGGIE

Mm. Is there a Mrs. Joshua?

PETER

Yes, but we are divorced.

REGGIE

Oh, that wasn't a proposal. I'm just curious.

PETER

Is your husband with you?

REGGIE

Oh, no. Charles is never with me. What do people call you, Pete?

PETER

Mr. Joshua.

(turning to go)

I've enjoyed talking with you.

REGGIE

Now you're angry.

PETER

No, no. I'm not angry. I just have a lot of parking to do. I'm going back to Paris too.

REGGIE

But wasn't it Shakespeare who said when strangers do meet in far off lands, they should ere long see each other again.

PETER

Shakespeare never said that.

REGGIE

How do you know?

BRIAN

It's terrible. You just made it up.

REGGIE

Well, it sounds right. You're gonna call me.

BRIAN

Are you in the book?

REGGIE

Well, Charles is.

BRIAN

Is there only one Charles Lampert?

Close shot—Reggie, her face clouding.

REGGIE

Hmm. Lord, I hope so.

EXT. AVENUE FOCH—LAMPERT APARTMENT HOUSE—DAY

The Arc de Triomphe at the far end of the Avenue. Camera pans to pick up a taxi as it pulls up before the handsome building. Inside are Reggie, Sylvie and Jean-Louis.

Med. shot—taxi—Lampert Apartment House as Reggie climbs out and the driver begins unloading her suitcases.

REGGIE

Goodbye Sylvie, and thanks.

(she turns toward the house)

Jean-Louis sticks his head out of the taxi window.

JEAN-LOUIS

When you get your divorce, are you going back to America?

REGGIE

Well, don't you want me to stay?

JEAN-LOUIS

Yes, of course, but if you went back, you could write me a letter.

REGGIE

You could have the stamps. I'll get you some here, okay?

JEAN-LOUIS

Okay.

REGGIE

Goodbye.

Reggie walks toward the house with the driver, who carries her cases. She presses the button that electrically opens the front door.

INT. APARTMENT LANDING—DAY

As the elevator rises Reggie gets out, followed by the driver. He puts down the bags in front of the apartment door.

REGGIE

(handing him a tip)

Merci.

The driver leaves. She inserts the key and turns it.

INT. LAMPERT APARTMENT—ENTRANCE HALL—DAY

Door opens and Reggie steps inside. She stops, her expression changing.

Reverse shot from Reggie's p.o.v. as the camera pans the entrance hall. It is bare—no furniture, no rug, no pictures, no nothing.

INT. LAMPERT APARTMENT—DAY

As Reggie hurries into the entrance hall.

REGGIE

Honorine—!

No answer.

Now, camera following, she goes into the Salon. It is also empty—stripped bare. There are squares of the wall's original color where paintings used to hang, the hooks still in the wall.

REGGIE

Honorine? Honorine!

She rushes now, going into the bedroom, camera following crazily, lurching and careening behind her. The bedroom, too, is empty. She goes to the built-in wardrobe closets and throws open all the doors. Only some hangers remain. She pulls open the drawers—nothing!

She turns, and running now, goes through another door to the library, camera following. The rows of shelves are as empty as the rest of the apartment. She begins to turn in a circle, looking for something, anything. In a panic she turns and runs out, colliding suddenly with a man whom she (and we) have not noticed until the moment of impact.

Reggie screams.

Close shot—inspector grandpierre, a heavy-set man of no particular age with tobacco-colored hair and a mustache.

GRANDPIERRE

Madame Charles Lampert?

Wider angle including Reggie, in a state of near-shock.

REGGIE

Yes.

INT. MORGUE—DAY

We see a large metal drawer being opened and an all-too-familiar shape outlined under a damp sheet of muslin.

Another angle—overhead, looking straight down at the tops of Reggie's, Grandpierre's and an Attendant's head and smack into the open drawer.

Grandpierre lifts a corner of the sheet at the bottom and reveals a bare foot with a ticket tied to its big toe.

He stoops to read it. Satisfied, he recovers the foot, then moves to the other end to uncover the head. As the sheet starts to lift:

Reverse shot, Reggie as she looks down into the camera. She closes her eyes for a moment, then looks again.

GRANDPIERRE (O.S.)

Well, Madame—?

She nods.

GRANDPIERRE (O.S.)

You are positive?

She nods again. Grandpierre moves into the shot.

GRANDPIERRE

You loved him?

REGGIE

I'm very cold.

Grandpierre nods as he turns to the unseen attendant.

Camera suddenly moves as the 'drawer' is slid back into the wall. Blackness comes with a loud clang and continues while the echo dies.

INT. GRANDPIERRE'S OFFICE—DAY

Close shot—desk drawer (from above) as it is pulled open. A photograph of Charles Lampert lies face up in the drawer. A hand reaches in and pulls it out.

Wider angle, including Grandpierre sitting behind his desk, and Reggie, sitting across from him. The office is as bare as most policemen's offices. Grandpierre studies the photo.

GRANDPIERRE

We discovered your husband's body lying next to the tracks of the Paris–Bordeaux railroad line. He was dressed only in his pajamas. Do you know of any reason why he might have wanted to leave France?

REGGIE

Leave? No.

GRANDPIERRE

Your husband possessed a ticket of passage on the Maranguape. It sailed for Venezuela this morning at seven.

REGGIE

I'm very confused.

She starts to rummage through her bag. Grandpierre shoves a package of French cigarettes across the desk to her. But she pulls a package of nuts out of her bag. She begins separating the shells with her thumb nail and eating the nuts, depositing the shells in the ashtray. Grandpierre watches this for an instant.

GRANDPIERRE

He was American. Your husband?

REGGIE

Swiss.

GRANDPIERRE

Ah, Swiss. His profession?

REGGIE

He didn't have one.

GRANDPIERRE

He was a wealthy man?

REGGIE

I suppose so. I don't know.

GRANDPIERRE

About how wealthy would you say?

REGGIE

I don't know.

GRANDPIERRE

Where did he keep his money?

REGGIE

I don't know.

GRANDPIERRE

Beside yourself, who is his nearest relative?

REGGIE

I don't know.

GRANDPIERRE

(exploding)

That's absurd, madam. Totally absurd.

REGGIE

I know.

(pause)

I'm sorry.

GRANDPIERRE

It is all right.

Grandpierre sighs, puts down his pencil and pushes a button on the desk. He removes a cigar from his desk and inserts it into his mouth.

REGGIE

I wish you wouldn't.

He rips the cigar out of his mouth and slams it back into the drawer, closing it fiercely. Grandpierre picks up the phone.

GRANDPIERRE

(speaking into the phone)

Les effets de Lampert.

GRANDPIERRE

(to Reggie)

On Wednesday last, your husband sold the entire contents of the apartment at public auction. Everything. The gallery paid him $1,250,000 new francs, in dollars, a quarter of a million. The authorities in Bordeaux searched this compartment on the train. They searched it thoroughly. They did not find $250,000.

A uniformed policeman enters, places a Lufthansa bag on Grandpierre's desk, leaves and closes the door.

These few things are all that was found in the train compartment. There was no other baggage. Your husband must have been in a great hurry. One wallet containing $4,000 francs. One agenda. His last notation was made yesterday, Thursday, 5:00 PM Jardin des Champs-Elysees. Why there?

REGGIE

I don't know. Perhaps he met somebody.

GRANDPIERRE

Obviously. One ticket of passage to South America. One letter, stamp but unsealed, addressed to you.

REGGIE

May I see it, please?

Grandpierre hands Reggie the letter, she sits and reads it aloud:

"My dear Regina, I hope you are enjoying your holiday. Megeve can be so lovely at this time of year. The days pass very slowly and I hope to see you soon as always. Charles. PS, your dentist called yesterday. Your appointment has been changed."

Not much is it?

GRANDPIERRE

We took the liberty of calling your dentist. We thought perhaps we would learn something.

REGGIE

Did you?

GRANDPIERRE

Yes. Your appointment has been changed.

He opens the desk drawer, puts the cigar back in his mouth and lights a match by scratching it against the glass desktop before he remembers Reggie's request. He puts it back in the drawer again and details the items in the bag.

One key to your apartment. One comb, one fountain pen, one toothbrush, one tin of tooth powder. That is all. If you will sign this list, you may take the things with you.

REGGIE

Is that all? May I leave now?

GRANDPIERRE

One more question. Is this your husband's passport?

He reaches into the desk drawer and pulls out a passport which he hands to her.

Insert—passport, the cover indicates that it is Swiss. Reggie's hand opens it to a picture of a man—the man we saw in Grandpierre's photo. Under it is the name: *CHARLES LAMPERT*.

Med. shot—reggie and grandpierre

REGGIE

Of course it is.

GRANDPIERRE

And this?

He hands her another passport.

Insert—second passport, the cover is American. When it is opened, we see the identical picture, but the name under it reads: *CHARLES VOSS*.

Med. Shot—Reggie and Grandpierre

REGGIE

I don't understand.

GRANDPIERRE

And this?

Insert—third passport, Italian, which when opened shows the same photo with the name *CARLO FABRI.*

And this?

Insert—fourth passport, Venezuelan, the same photo, and the name *CARLOS MORENO.*

Reggie stares at Grandpierre, nervously eating candies.

INT. LAMPERT APARTMENT—DUSK

The house is empty as before. Now it is silent, the late afternoon light putting Reggie in shadow. She stands by the fireplace, looking wistful, smoking. Suddenly there is the noise of the door buzzer and footsteps.

Closer shot—Reggie, illuminated as the door opens in front of her. She's surprised.

Another angle as Peter enters.

PETER

Oh, I telephoned, but nobody answered.

REGGIE

Hello.

PETER

Hello. I wanted to tell you how sorry I am and see if there's anything I can do.

REGGIE

How did you find out?

PETER

It's in the afternoon papers. I'm very sorry.

REGGIE

Thank you.

PETER

Uh. I pressed the bell, but it isn't ringing. I guess.

REGGIE

I know there's no electricity.

PETER

Well, where did everything go?

REGGIE

Charles sold it all to auction. This is all I have left. I love this room, but Charles never really saw it. Only the things in it. I think I preferred it this way.

PETER

What are you going to do?

REGGIE

Try and get my old job back at EURESCO, I suppose.

PETER

Doing what?

REGGIE

I'm a simultaneous translator like Sylvie. Only she's English into French, and I'm French into English. That's what I was doing before I married Charles. The police probably think I killed him.

PETER

Instant divorce. You mean?

REGGIE

Something like that. It's terrible. It ended this way though. Tossed off a train like a sack of third class mail.

PETER

Well, come on. You can't stay here.

REGGIE

I don't know where to go.

PETER

We'll find you a hotel.

REGGIE

Nothing too expensive. I'm not a lady of leisure anymore, you know?

PETER

Something clean and modest and near enough to EURESCO so that you can take a cab when it rains. Okay?

REGGIE

Okay

INT. FUNERAL CHAPEL—DAY

Close shot of a phonograph. A hand appears, starts the record on it spinning, then places the arm at the beginning. An instant later organ music starts with a roar.

INT. FUNERAL CHAPEL—DAY

Close shot of the coffin. It rests on a low platform, with a bouquet or two of flowers near the head, the lid open.

Inside, the face made up to look lifelike (but failing), lie the remnants of Charles Lampert.

Close shot—Grandpierre. The inspector sits quietly, eyes downcast, staring at his hands in a prayer-like attitude. Camera pulls back, revealing row after row of empty wooden bench-like seats in the large, dimly-lit, high-ceilinged room. Finally, in the first row, Reggie and Sylvie are discovered. Besides Grandpierre, they are the only ones present. Reggie turns around to look at the empty room. They speak in whispers.

REGGIE

Okay. Not a very large turnout is it?

SYLVIE

Didn't Charles have any friends?

REGGIE

Don't ask me. I'm only the widow.

(indicating Grandpierre)

If Charles had died in bed, we wouldn't even have him.

SYLVIE

At least he knows how to behave at funerals.

Close shot—Grandpierre, his eyes still lowered. Camera pans down to feature his hands—he is methodically trimming his nails with a small clipper.

Two shot—Sylvie and Reggie.

SYLVIE

Have you no idea who could have done it?

REGGIE

Until two days ago, the only thing I really knew about Charles was his name. Now it seems I didn't even know that.

The front door of the chapel is heard opening and a shaft of daylight streams in. The women turn.

Med. shot—chapel door. The short, slender figure of a man is outlined against the bright outdoor light. He stands for a moment, then closes the door after him. Leopold Gideon, bald, in his middle forties, wearing thick glasses, glances around nervously, like a barnyard bird. Then he walks down one of the side aisles of the Chapel.

Close shot—grandpierre as he watches Gideon.

Close shot—reggie as she watches him.

Med. shot—the bier.

Gideon arrives at the coffin. He stops, looks down at Lampert's body for a moment. Then, suddenly, in rapid succession, he sneezes six times. He takes a small bottle from his pocket, shakes a pill from it and swallows it dry.

Two shot—Reggie and Sylvie

SYLVIE

He must have known Charles pretty well.

REGGIE

How can you tell?

SYLVIE

He's allergic to him.

REGGIE

Never seen him before.

Gideon turns and walks back up the aisle. He sneezes as he passes Reggie.

REGGIE

Bless you.

Gideon, staring back at Reggie, stumbles and winds up face to face with Grandpierre. He stops, turns and takes a seat across the aisle.

SYLVIE

Do you know him?

REGGIE

Never seen him before.

Sylvie turns and glances at Gideon. Again, the sound of the door opening interrupts them. They turn to look.

Med. shot—chapel door.

Again the figure of a man is outlined in silhouette against the outside brightness. When he closes the door we can see "Tex" Penthollow, a slim, rangy man with sandy-colored hair, a weatherbeaten face, blue eyes—also in his forties. He wears a velvet-corduroy suit, string tie and a bright yellow flower in his lapel. A Bull Durham tag hangs from his outside breast pocket, dangling from its string.

He starts down the aisle toward the bier, the camera leading him.

Med. shot—the bier as Tex arrives. He stands staring at Lampert's body, produces a small mirror from inside his jacket and puts it beneath Lampert's nose. Once his death is confirmed, Tex then takes the flower from his lapel and throws it into the open box.

Close shot—Tex

TEX

(heavy Texas accent)

Arrivaderci, Charlie.

Wider angle as Tex turns away from the coffin and approaches Reggie and Sylvie, addressing the latter—after having first reached for his hat which he discovers he isn't wearing.

Uh, Ms. Lampert, ma'am, Charlie had no call of doing it that way. No siree.

Tex nods his head and moves off to find a seat. He ignores Gideon as he sits across the aisle from him.

REGGIE

What next?

Med. shot—chapel door.

It flies open, this time with a bang, and the large MAN who appears almost fills the frame.

Closer shot—Tex as the loud noise awakens him with a snort, mid-snore.

Med. shot—closing the door, we see Herman Scobie, a heavyweight—tall and wide, but not fat—with thinning blonde hair combed straight back. About the same age as the first two men, Scobie is dressed in a battered raincoat, his hands thrust deep in the pockets. He marches down the aisle. Looking straight ahead, camera panning with him. He stops before the coffin and stares into it.

Close shot—Scobie as he stares down into the coffin, his tongue trying to dislodge a bit of food caught in his teeth. He stares hard at the body, squinting his eyes. Then he removes one hand from his pocket, removes a pin from the inside of his lapel, picks his teeth with it, then slowly lets the hand down, into the coffin.

Close shot—Scobie's hand, the pin held between thumb and forefinger, he jabs it slowly but positively deep into the back of one of the dead man's hands. There is no reaction.

Close shot—Scobie watches the dead man carefully, still squinting. Finally satisfied, he returns the pin to his lapel and walks back up the aisle and out of the door, slamming it after him.

Close shot—Reggie, having watched Scobie exit. Suddenly a hand falls on her shoulder. She jumps in alarm and utters a little cry of fright.

MESSENGER

Mille pardon, Madame.

REGGIE

Merci.

MESSENGER

Pardon . . . pardon . . .

He backs off and is gone. Reggie looks at the letter, back and front, then starts to open it.

SYLVIE

Who's it from?

REGGIE

The American Embassy.

She pulls out the letter and starts to read it.

Insert—the letter bears the Great Seal as a letterhead and the typed message reads:

Dear Mrs. Lampert: Please drop by my office tomorrow at noon-thirty. I am anxious to discuss the matter of your late husband's death. Sincerely, H. Bartholomew.

Two shot—Reggie and Sylvie. Sylvie has been reading over Reggie's shoulder.

EXT. THE AMERICAN EMBASSY—ESTABLISHING—DAY

A fine old building in the Rue Gabriel.

INT. EMBASSY CORRIDOR—DAY

As Reggie leaves the elevator two young diplomatic types step in, immersed in conversation.

1ST DIPLOMAT

I bluffed the Old Man out of the last pot—with a pair of deuces.

2ND DIPLOMAT

What's so depressing about that?

1ST DIPLOMAT

Well I mean if I can do it, what are the Russians doing to him?

The elevator door closes on them. Reggie reacts to this and starts down the hall, finally stopping at the door.

Med. shot—a door marked *307-A H. BARTHOLOMEW.* Reggie knocks then opens the door.

INT. BARTHOLOMEW'S OUTER OFFICE—DAY

The office is empty, the typewriter on the secretary's desk is covered with its plastic shroud. Reggie enters, looks for somebody, notices that the door to the private office is slightly ajar.

REGGIE

(tentatively)

Hello—?

(there is no answer)

Hello?

BARTHOLOMEW (O.S.)

(from the private office)

Is there anything wrong, Miss Tompkins?

Bartholomew comes to the door and looks in. He has a hangdog face and looks, on first examination, older than his forty-odd years.

REGGIE

Uh, Ms. Tompkins isn't here.

BARTHOLOMEW

Oh, I'm sorry. My secretary must have gone to lunch. Uh, you are?

REGGIE

Mrs. Lampert, Mrs. Charles Lampert.

BARTHOLOMEW

Oh, yes. Please, uh, come in, Mrs. Lampert.

He motions for her to enter, standing aside to let her do so.

Excuse me for a moment, Mrs. Lampert.

A can of lighter fluid stands open on the desk and a crumpled hankie beside it.

BARTHOLOMEW

Excuse me for a moment, Mrs. Lampert—it's a stubborn little devil.

As Reggie enters, he follows, taking a can of lighter fluid and a hankie from the radiator beside the door. He starts working at a stain on his necktie.

It's a stubborn little devil. Dry cleaning wise, things are all fouled up. I had a good man, a really excellent man on the Rue Ponthieu. But HQ asked us to use the plant here in the building to ease the gold outflow.

REGGIE

Mr. Bartholomew, are you quite sure you know who I am?

BARTHOLOMEW

(looking up)

You're Charles Lampert's widow, yes? I'm very sorry.

(going back to the tie)

Last time I sent out a tie, only the spot came back. Voilà, as they say... Won't you sit down, Mrs. Lampert?

Med. shot—Reggie sits as Bartholomew takes a small basket from a cabinet and goes to his desk.

I've got something here... I've got liverwurst, liverwurst, chicken and liverwurst.

REGGIE

No. Thank you.

BARTHOLOMEW

Mrs. Lampert, do you know what CIA is?

REGGIE

I don't suppose it's an airline. Is it?

CARSON

Central Intelligence Agency, CIA.

REGGIE

You mean spies and all of that?

CARSON

Only we call them agents.

REGGIE

We? You mean you?

Bartholomew starts uncorking a bottle of wine.

BARTHOLOMEW

Someone has to do it, Mrs. Lampert.

REGGIE

It's just that I didn't think people like you are supposed to admit—

BARTHOLOMEW

Oh, I'm not an agent. I'm an administrator, a desk jockey, trying to run a bureau of overworked men with under-allocated—

(pulls out the cork)

—funds. Congress seems to think that all a spy needs—

REGGIE

Agent.

BARTHOLOMEW

Yes. That all he needs is a codebook, a cyanide pill, and he's in business.

REGGIE

What's all this got to do with me, Mr. Bartholomew?

BARTHOLOMEW

Your husband was wanted by the United States government.

REGGIE

(quietly)

May I have a sandwich please?

CARSON

Chicken or Liverwurst?

REGGIE

Chicken.

He comes around to bring her the sandwich and sits on his desk in front of her.

BARTHOLOMEW

To be more specific, Mrs. Lampert, your husband was wanted by this agency.

REGGIE

So that was it?

BARTHOLOMEW

Yes, we of course knew him by his real name, Voss. Charles Voss.

(taking a photo from his desk)

Alright, Mrs. Voss. Now I'd like you to look at this photograph here for a moment, please, tell us if you recognize—

(indicating a photo on the desk)

Oh, by the way, have you seen this one? Scott, Kathy and Ham Jr.

REGGIE

Very sweet.

BARTHOLOMEW

Aren't they? All right, Mrs. Voss.

REGGIE

Please stop calling me that. Lampert's the name on the marriage license.

BARTHOLOMEW

Oh, I'm terribly sorry. Mrs. Lampert, would you look at that photograph and tell me if you recognize anyone, please? Just a moment. Have a good look.

He reaches back into the drawer and pulls out a glass which he gives her.

Close shot—photo of FOUR MEN, all in army uniform, sitting behind a table. The glass is held over the first, magnifying the face.

Closer shot—photo of a young CHARLES LAMPERT.

REGGIE'S VOICE (O.S.)

It's Charles!

BARTHOLOMEW'S VOICE (O.S.)

Very good.

Med. shot.

REGGIE

He looked so young. When was this taken?

CARSON

1944. Next please.

The glass and the camera move to the next man—a young TEX.

REGGIE

A man who was at the funeral yesterday. A tall man in a corduroy suit.

BARTHOLOMEW

Does the name Tex Panthollow mean anything to you?

REGGIE

No.

BARTHOLOMEW

Do you like some wine?

REGGIE

No, thank you.

BARTHOLOMEW

Next please.

The glass and the camera move to the third face—a young Gideon.

REGGIE

He was there too. A little less hair, but it's the same one.

BARTHOLOMEW

Do you know him, Mrs. Lampert? Leopold W. Gideon?

REGGIE

No.

BARTHOLOMEW

The last one, please.

The glass and camera move to the fourth face—a young Scobie.

REGGIE

That's a face you don't forget. He was there too!

BARTHOLOMEW

Herman Scobie. You've never seen him before either?

REGGIE

No, thank heaven.

Med. shot—Reggie and Bartholomew

BARTHOLOMEW

Mrs. Lambert, I'm very much afraid that you are in a great deal of danger.

REGGIE

Why should I be in any danger?

BARTHOLOMEW

You are Charles Voss' wife. Now that he's dead, you are their only lead.

REGGIE

Mr. Bartholomew, if you're trying to frighten me, you're doing a first rate job.

BARTHOLOMEW

Please do what we ask, Mrs. Lampert. It's your only chance.

REGGIE

Gladly. But I don't know what you want. You haven't told me.

BARTHOLOMEW

Oh, I haven't? Well, it's the money, Mrs. Lampert, the money.

(mouth full)

The $250,000 Charles Voss received from the auction. Those three men want it, too. They want it very badly.

REGGIE

But that's Charles' money, not theirs.

BARTHOLOMEW

Oh, Mrs. Lampert, I'd love to see you try and convince them of that. Oh my.

REGGIE

But then whose is it? His or theirs?

BARTHOLOMEW

Ours.

REGGIE

Oh.

BARTHOLOMEW

Charles Voss stole $250,000 from the United States government. I'm afraid we want it back.

REGGIE

But I don't have it.

BARTHOLOMEW

That's impossible, Mrs. Lampert. You're the only one who could have it.

REGGIE

Mr. Bartholomew. If I had a quarter of a million dollars, believe me, I'd know it.

BARTHOLOMEW

Nevertheless, Mrs. Lampert, you've got it.

REGGIE

You mean it's just lying around somewhere? All that cash?

BARTHOLOMEW

Or a certified check, a safe deposit, key, baggage claim . . . You look for it, Mrs. Lampert, I'm quite sure you'll find it.

REGGIE

But—

BARTHOLOMEW

(cutting her off, urgent)

Look for it. Look just as hard and as fast as you can. You may not have a great deal of time. Those three men know you've got the money just as surely as we do. You won't be safe until the money is in our hands. Is that clear?

REGGIE nods. He writes something on a pad of paper and tears it off, handing it to her.

Now, here's where you ought to call me, day or night. It's a direct line to both my office and my apartment. And please don't tell anyone about coming to see us today. It could prove fatal for them as well as yourself. As I said, Mrs. Lampert, I'm afraid you're in a great deal of danger. I regret very much having to say this, but please remember what happened to your husband.

EXT. ESPLANADE DES CHAMPS-ELYÉES—DAY

Med. shot—Guignol. One of the French Punch and Judy shows set up on certain days in the small park alongside the broad avenue between the Rond Point and the Place de la Concorde. At the moment, Judy, as always, is beating Punch with a bat. The sound of children laughing and screaming can be heard.

Various close shots of children sitting on small benches lined up to face the stage. Their attention is fixed on the show, their belief totally suspended by the play as only children's can be—laughing at the slapstick, booing the villain, frightened by the perils.

Med. shot—Reggie sitting on the last bench, next to some children. They are laughing but she isn't—she just watches, her attention caught up but her face void of emotion. The bench is too low for her, forcing her knees up almost under her chin.

After a moment, Peter comes up behind her and, stepping over the benches, sits beside her. She doesn't seem to notice.

Throughout the following scene the children and the actors can be heard in the b.g.

PETER

Hello?

She turns and looks at him for a moment.

REGGIE

Hello, Peter.

PETER

Now didn't you telephone me to meet you on that corner over there?

REGGIE

I'm sorry, I heard the children laughing.

A roar from the children. Reggie and Peter turn toward the stage.

Med. shot—Guignol, Punch and Judy are arguing loudly.

Two shot—Reggie and Peter

REGGIE

Do you understand French?

PETER

Not a word. I'm still having trouble with English.

REGGIE

The man and the woman are married.

Close Shot—Guignol Stage, Punch and Judy are fighting with sticks.

PETER

Oh, I can see that. They're batting each other over the head

Finally, Judy knocks Punch out of sight and a puppet wearing a three-cornered hat appears.

PETER

Who's that with the hat?

Med shot—Grandpierre wearing a hat, he stands off in the background, watching.

REGGIE

That's the policeman. He wants to arrest Judy for killing Punch.

Close shot—Guignol Stage, Judy and the policeman are batting one another.

PETER

What's she saying now?

REGGIE

That she's innocent, she didn't do it.

PETER

Oh, she did it. All right.

REGGIE

I believe her.

Punch's head appears on the other side of the stage, says something, then ducks out.

PETER

Well, who was that?

REGGIE

That's Punch, of course.

Two shot—Reggie and Peter

PETER

Punch, of course, I thought he was dead.

REGGIE

He's only pretending to teach her a lesson. Only he is dead, Peter, I saw him, he's not pretending. Somebody threw him off a train. Charles was mixed up in something terrible. What am I going to do?

PETER

I wish you'd let me help you. It doesn't sound like the sort of thing a young woman can handle by herself.

Close shot—Guignol Stage. Judy has gotten the upper hand is now batting the policeman's brains out.

Close shot—Grandpierre as he winces.

Two shot—Reggie and Peter

PETER

How about making me vice-president in charge of cheering you up?

REGGIE

(jumping at the suggestion)

Starting tonight?

INT. NIGHTCLUB—NIGHT

Med. shot—Emcee. He stands on the dance floor in front of a five piece Latin dance band, a spotlight on him, wearing his professional smile as he speaks into a mike.

EMCEE

Bonsoir mesdames et messieurs, good evening ladies and gentlemen, *guten Abend, meine Damen und Herren—ce soir, comme tous les soirs, l'attraction ici, au Black Sheep Club, c'est vous! Venez, mesdames et messieurs,* step right up, ladies and gentlemen, *kommen Sie her, meine Damen en Herren, avanti, signore e signori—avanti!*

Med. shot—Reggie and Peter at their table. Reggie is dressed in a lovely Givenchy dress.

PETER

What's going on?

REGGIE

Fun games. Evidently, we are the floorshow. Come on.

PETER

What? You and me?

She rises and pulls him towards the stage.

EMCEE

Avante. Avante. Senore and Senori . . . Ecoutez-moi bien Listen to me, ladies and gentlemen.

The Emcee brings a stout middle-aged woman to the stage and positions her face to face with a younger woman as the other patrons look on.

Listen to me. The rules of the game are very simple. There are two teams. And for each team there is one orange. For every team, there is one orange, *una naranja,* and like so—

He places the orange beneath each woman's chin and pushes their heads down to secure them.

you pass the orange to the person behind you s*ans vous servir de vos mains*—without the use of your hands. Are you ready? *Uno. Due, Tre.*

Close shot—the Emcee blows a whistle.

Two shot—Peter and middle-aged woman

Peter attempts to take the orange from her, making several awkward tries before the orange starts to slip down the Woman's front. He goes after it and winds up with his face in her bosom, while Reggie looks on eagerly. Slapstick comedy ensues as he struggles to claim the orange.

The other team, starting with a middle aged man and the young woman, are having more success, the man grasping it and beginning the process of passing it on to another woman. Finally Peter manages to grasp the orange beneath his chin, to pass it on to Reggie.

They go at it, working their bodies together to make it all possible. Then, for a moment, the game and the onlookers seem less important than their proximity. But, alas, they are too good despite themselves and the transfer is accomplished—again with appreciative cheers from the team.

Reggie, with the orange now tucked firmly under her chin, turns to the next team-member in line and is locked in an embrace before she realizes her partner is Leopold Gideon, the short, balding man seen at the funeral and later in Bartholomew's photo.

Reggie starts to draw back but Gideon holds her tightly. Putting his chin around the orange he is able to speak quietly in Reggie's ear.

Close two shot—Reggie and Gideon

Her eyes show her fright as he whispers:

GIDEON

Mrs. Lampert?

REGGIE

Who are you?

GIDEON

Didn't Charles tell you, Mrs. Lampert?

REGGIE

Tell me what?

GIDEON

It doesn't belong to you. You do know that, don't you?

REGGIE

I don't know anything.

GIDEON

(sharply)

Mrs. Lampert—any morning now you could wake up dead, Mrs. Lampert.

REGGIE

Leave me alone!

GIDEON

Dead, Mrs. Lampert. Like last week's news—like Charles, Mrs. Lampert.

REGGIE

(shouting)

Stop it!

Close shot—Reggie's and Gideon's feet as Reggie hauls off and kicks Gideon full in the shin.

Close shot—Gideon, who stiffens as the pain registers. Instead of shouting he merely closes his eyes.

Wider angle, including Reggie and Gideon and Peter standing by, as well as some spectators. Peter comes quickly forward.

PETER

What's the trouble?

REGGIE

He stepped on my foot.

GIDEON

(cringing)

Forgive me.

REGGIE

(grabbing her things from the table)

Wait here. I won't be long.

She runs off toward the rear of the club.

GIDEON

It was quite unintentional. I'm sure

INT. NIGHTCLUB LOUNGE—NIGHT

A small, dimly lit area with a door to the combination men's-women's room and a phonebooth with a solid door.

The music and shouting from upstairs float down. Reggie comes down the stairs and goes to the 'phone, flicking on the light and closing the door after her.

INT. PHONE BOOTH—NIGHT

Reggie takes a *jeton* ('phone token') from her bag and drops it in the slot. Then she takes out a slip of paper (the one given her by Bartholomew) and dials the number written on it. She listens to it ring, then evidently he answers.

REGGIE

(into phone)

Mr. Bartholomew, this is Reggie Lampert. Mr. Bartholomew, I just saw one of those men . . .

(she stops)

Mr. Bartholomew, can you hear me? Mr. Bartholomew, this is Reggie Lampert, I just . . .

Suddenly the door of the booth opens and Reggie wheels to look, slamming the receiver down as she does.

REVERSE SHOT—PHONE BOOTH—NIGHT

Tex Penthollow, the second man from the funeral (and photo), the man in the corduroy suit and string tie, stands in the doorway, his face calm, a hand-rolled but unlit cigarette in his mouth. He has put one foot up against the side of the door so she can't leave. Reggie stares at him, terrified.

TEX

Howdy.

REGGIE

What do you want?

Tex takes a book of matches from his pocket.

TEX

Now, you must be kidding.

REGGIE

No, I'm not.

TEX

Come on now, Ms. Lampert. You know what it is. You're gonna get it for me too because you know I ain't fooling around here. No sirree bob.

He strikes a match and lights his cigarette, holding the burning match in his hand afterward.

REGGIE

(terrified)

No, please stop!

Tex lights another match and throws it into her lap. She beats this one out too.

TEX

Now don't make too much noise, Ms. Lampert.

He lights another match and reaches out toward her hair with it. She shrinks back.

TEX

It could get a whole lot worse, you know.

Then he throws it into her lap. As he continues to speak he punctuates each phrase or so with another lit match. Reggie is too busy beating them out to do anything else.

TEX

It belongs to me, Ms. Lampert, and you're going to get it for me, or your life ain't going to be worth a paper it's printed on. You seeing what I'm saying to you?

REGGIE

Stop! Stop! Please stop!

TEX

Now you go home and think it over real careful right now.

Tex leaves, closing the door of the booth behind him. Reggie, shaking, closes her eyes and puts a lollipop in her mouth to calm herself. The door opens and Peter enters.

PETER

What's the matter? What are you doing in here?

REGGIE

(in a carefully annunciated way)

I'm having a nervous breakdown.

INT. HOTEL LOBBY–NIGHT

Reggie and Peter enter the lobby and pass by the Night Porter, sleeping in one of the chairs. He follows her as she claims her room key as they talk.

PETER

Now, hold it–I waited long enough. What happened back there?

REGGIE

I'm not sure if I'm supposed to tell you or not.

PETER

What does that mean?

REGGIE

He said if I told anybody, it could prove fatal for them as well as for me.

PETER

Who said?

REGGIE

That's what I'm not supposed to say!

PETER

Now stop that nonsense!

REGGIE

Stop bullying me. Everybody's bullying me.

PETER

I'm not bullying you.

REGGIE

Yes, you were. You said it was nonsense. Being murdered in cold blood is not nonsense. Why don't you try it sometime?

(turns to face him)

Would you mind seeing me to the door?

PETER

Of course not.

INT. ELEVATOR—NIGHT

As Reggie and Peter enter the small cage. It is somewhat cramped, forcing them to stand close together.

REGGIE

It's a good place for making friends.

PETER

You said this afternoon your husband was mixed up in something.

(examining the cleft in his chin)

REGGIE

How do you shave in there?

PETER

What was it?

REGGIE

What was what?

PETER

What your husband was mixed up in.

REGGIE

Look, I know it's asking you to stretch your imagination, but don't you think you could pretend just for a moment that I'm a woman—

PETER

Now listen, I could already be arrested for transporting a minor above the first floor. Here you are.

REGGIE

Where?

PETER

On the street where you live.

REGGIE

How about once more around the park?

He reaches across her and opens the door.

PETER

How about getting out of here? Come on, child, out.

INT. HOTEL CORRIDOR THIRD LANDING—NIGHT

Reggie leaves the elevator, followed by Peter. They walk to her door.

REGGIE

Won't you come in for a minute?

PETER

No, I won't.

REGGIE

I don't bite, you know, unless it's called for.

PETER

How would you like a spanking?

REGGIE

How would you like a punch in the nose? Stop treating me like a child.

PETER

Well, then stop behaving like one. Now if you want to tell me what's troubling you, fine. If not, I'm tired. It's late and I want to go home to bed. Oh . . .

The elevator descends, leaving him stranded.

REGGIE

Do you know what's wrong with you?

BRIAN

No. What?

REGGIE

Nothing.

INT. REGGIE'S ROOM—NIGHT

Reggie enters a dark room, turns on the light and screams. Standing in the center is Herman Scobie, the large man in the battered raincoat.

SCOBIE

Where is it, lady?

REGGIE

I don't know.

He starts slowly advancing toward Reggie. She looks down.

Close shot—Instead of a human hand Scobie has a twin-pronged metal claw.

Wider angle—Scobie sees where Reggie is staring; looks down at it himself, then lunges at her, raising the hand to strike.

SCOBIE

I want it. Give it to me. It's mine.

The hand is starting to come down. Reggie, moving quickly, turns and flees back into the hallway.

INT. HOTEL CORRIDOR THIRD LANDING—NIGHT

As Reggie slams the door behind her, the metal claw crashes against the wooden panel inside the door and splinters through it, visible on this side now. Reggie turns and runs down the stairs.

REGGIE

(screaming)

Peter! Peter! A man tried to kill me.

Peter comes running up the stairs. He passes her, sees the metal hand through the door, and enters her room.

Close shot of Reggie as she hides behind the corner of the stairwell, listening to Peter and Scobie fight. The noise subsides and she hears a window open. She approaches, slowly, opens the door and goes inside.

INT. REGGIE'S ROOM—NIGHT

Wide shot—Her room is a shambles, empty of people.

REGGIE

(entering cautiously)

Peter—?

Slowly Peter's hand appears from behind the bed, shaking groggily. Reggie rushes to him and helps him sit on the bed.

Oh, Peter—are you hurt?

PETER

I sprained my pride. How are you?

REGGIE

Scared.

PETER

You'll be all right. Where did it go?

REGGIE

Out the window, I guess.

PETER

Lock the door, and don't let anyone in except me. And close these windows after me.

REGGIE

Be careful.

Peter goes, unsteady on his feet, to the window and looks out. He then turns back.

PETER

(one leg over the sill)

You just took the words right out of my mouth.

He climbs out.

EXT. HOTEL WINDOW THIRD FLOOR—NIGHT

Outside the window to Reggie's room is a small, false balcony, consisting mostly of railing, with barely enough room between it and the building's facade for a man to stand. Peter appears and looks down over the railing.

EXT. HOTEL SIDEWALK (FROM ABOVE)—NIGHT

Looking straight down, there's no one on the street and it is too far to jump.

Med. shot—Peter is on the balcony, looking around. Reggie's is the last such balcony on one side, but there are two or three on the other.

Peter climbs over the railing and, holding on to it with one hand, reaches for the railing on the next balcony.

Close shot—Peter's hand as it stretches for the railing; it is several inches short of touching it.

Med. shot—Peter as he straightens up and prepares to jump.

EXT. HOTEL FACADE—NIGHT

Looking up from the street—Peter, high above, jumps to the next balcony.

Med. shot—Peter as he climbs over the railing of the second balcony. He sees a light coming through the window and looks in.

WOMAN'S VOICE (O.S.)

Alistair!

MAN'S VOICE (O.S.)

What is it now, Pamela?

WOMAN'S VOICE (O.S.)

It happened again! Another strange man peered in the window at me, but then went away!

MAN'S VOICE (O.S.)

Bad luck, Pamela.

EXT. HOTEL FACADE—NIGHT

Looking up from the street as Peter jumps to the next balcony.

Med. shot—Peter as he climbs over the rail to the third balcony. There is a light coming from this window, too. Peter looks in.

Med. shot—window—over Peter's shoulder. Inside the room are Gideon, Tex, and Scobie in the midst of a heated discussion.

GIDEON

That was a dumb move.

TEX

Man, and then some. It only he let us know he was going up to a room. We could have done something to keep him busy. Sneaking off of there that away by yourself. Man, what did you expect him to do, walk up and shake you by that hand of yours?

GIDEON

Yes, a dumb move, Herman. A dumb move!

INT. GIDEON'S HOTEL ROOM—NIGHT

PETER

Yes. It was a dumb move, Herman—what is the matter with you?

They all turn toward the window.

Wider angle as Peter climbs in through the window and joins them.

SCOBIE

Do you want some more?

GIDEON

Never mind that. Did you get the money?

PETER

How could I, with the three Marx Brothers breathing down my neck. I thought we had an agreement. Now, the girl trusts me. If she's got the money, I'll find out about it. But you just leave me alone.

SCOBIE

We took all the chances. The money belongs to us, not to him.

PETER

Now don't be piggy, Herman. A third of nothing is nothing. Just think about that, but make up your mind. She's waiting for me.

GIDEON

I don't see how another 24 hours could hurt anything.

TEX

Should've known after all these years.

SCOBIE

Then he gets it out of your share. Not mine. Not mine.

PETER

Either one of you got the room next to her?

TEX

Yeah, I have. Why?

PETER

Give me the key. Get yourself another room, I want to use it.

TEX

But if you do find that money, you ain't gonna forget to tell your buddies about it, are you?

PETER

Don't worry.

TEX

Oh no. I ain't worrying. You see this little fella here?

(puts his hand on Gideon's shoulder)

Oh, he worries, and he's even meaner than I am.

INT. HALLWAY—NIGHT

Peter goes to Reggie's room and knocks.

INT. REGGIE'S ROOM—NIGHT

Reggie is straightening up the room.

REGGIE

Who is it?

PETER

It's me, Peter.

Reggie unlocks the door and opens it. Peter enters and she closes the door again. They embrace, briefly.

PETER

There was no trace of him. Why don't you confide in me and tell me what this is all about?

REGGIE

There are three men. He's one of them. They think I have a quarter of a million dollars that belongs to them.

PETER

Go on.

REGGIE

That's all.

PETER

No, it isn't. Where's the money?

REGGIE

I don't know. They killed Charles to get it, but he must not have had it with him on the train.

PETER

So they think he left it with you?

REGGIE

But he didn't.

(tears welling)

I've looked everywhere, and if I don't find it, they're going to kill me.

PETER

No, they won't. I won't let them.

REGGIE

Peter, help me—you're the only one I can trust.

PETER

I'll help you. I told you I would. Come on . . .

She falls in his arms to be comforted.

REGGIE

Oh, I'm so hungry, I could faint. And I've gotten your suit all wet.

PETER

That's all right, it's a drip dry. Wipe your eyes.

REGGIE

Promise me you'll never lie to me the way Charles did. Why do people have to tell lies?

PETER

Usually it's because they want something. They're afraid the truth won't get it for them.

REGGIE

Do you tell lies?

A pause. The phone rings. Reggie answers it.

REGGIE

(into the phone)

Hello?

INT. OUTDOOR 'PHONE BOOTH—NIGHT

SCOBIE holds the receiver in his metal hand.

SCOBIE

Mrs. Lampert?. It's me, the man who was in your room a few minutes ago.

INT. REGGIE'S ROOM—NIGHT

REGGIE

(on the phone)

What do you want?

BRIAN

Who is it?

REGGIE

(whispering)

It's the man you had to fight with.

INT. PHONE BOOTH—NIGHT

SCOBIE

(on the phone)

Is Dyle with you?

INT. REGGIE'S ROOM—NIGHT

Close shot—Reggie

REGGIE

Who?

INT. PHONE BOOTH—NIGHT

SCOBIE

(on the phone)

The man who hit me, lady—Dyle—that's his name. What's wrong—is he still there?

INT. REGGIE'S ROOM—NIGHT

Reggie turns away from Peter so he can't see her face.

REGGIE

(on the phone)

Yes—that's right.

PETER

What's he saying?

INT. PHONE BOOTH—NIGHT

SCOBIE

(on the phone)

Don't trust him—don't tell him anything. He's after the money.

He hangs up.

INT. REGGIE'S ROOM—NIGHT

Slowly, Reggie lowers the phone from her ear and hangs it up. She hesitates a moment.

PETER

What was all that about?

REGGIE

He said if I don't give him the money, he'll kill me.

PETER

Oh, don't take it seriously. He's just trying to frighten you.

REGGIE

I believe what he said.

PETER

No, no, it's just a lot of words.

REGGIE

Words can hurt.

PETER

I know. Try to get some sleep.

(he pulls her close)

You'll feel better. And don't worry, I've arranged to take the room next door.

Reverse shot—Reggie looking over his shoulder, alarmed.

PETER

So you'll be all right. If you want anything, just bang on the wall. Better lock the door after me. Good night.

INT. HOTEL CORRIDOR—THIRD LANDING—NIGHT

Peter (now called Dyle) leaves Reggie's room and closes the door. He pauses, examining the hole Scobie made in it.

He goes towards his new room but doubles back, bends down and starts pulling at a loose thread in one of his socks. The thread unravels and, using his tie-pin, attaches one end of the thread to the bottom of Reggie's door. He then runs the thread along the floor to his door (next door) and works it underneath.

INT. REGGIE'S ROOM—NIGHT

Reggie is on the phone.

REGGIE

But I *am* calm, Mr. Bartholomew. What I'm trying to say is that there's someone else.

BARTHOLOMEW (V.O.)

What?

REGGIE

Someone who wasn't in that photograph you shown me today. He says his name is Peter Joshua. But it isn't—it's Dyle. Are you still there, Mr. Bartholomew?

INT. BARTHOLOMEW'S APARTMENT—NIGHT

Bartholomew on the phone. He is silent for a moment, his face troubled.

BARTHOLOMEW

Uh, yes. Yes, Mrs. Lampert. Uh, I don't know who this Mr. Dyle is, but it's just possible we were wrong about who killed your husband.

INT. REGGIE'S ROOM—NIGHT

REGGIE

You mean he might have? Mr. Bartholomew, I'm catching the next plane out of here. I . . . I'm not gonna sit around for somebody to make chopped liver out of me!

INT. BARTHOLOMEW'S APARTMENT—NIGHT

BARTHOLOMEW

Now take it easy, Mrs. Lampert—take it easy. Where are you now? Can you meet me at the market?

REGGIE (V.O.)

At Les Halles?

BARTHOLOMEW

Yes, opposite Saint-Eustache. I'll meet you there in 15 minutes.

INT. REGGIE'S ROOM—NIGHT

REGGIE

Alright. I'll be there in 15 minutes.

Reggie hangs up the phone, picks up her bag, checks her hair in the mirror, then starts for the door. She stops as she notices the connecting door leading to the room next door, DYLE's room. She goes to it, silently slips out the key and bends to peer through the keyhole.

INT. DYLE'S ROOM—NIGHT (THROUGH KEYHOLE)

Dyle is removing his coat. Before he lays it over a chair, he takes a gun from the inside pocket, checks it, and tucks it into his belt.

INT. DYLE'S ROOM—NIGHT

Close shot—room key, the thread attached to it is pulled (by the action of Reggie's door opening) and the key falls to the floor with a clatter.

Wide angle including DYLE as he reacts, his head wheeling to look at the key. Snatching his coat, he runs for the door.

INT. HOTEL CORRIDOR—THIRD LANDING—NIGHT

Reggie sneaks past Dyle's door. When she has passed, the door opens and Dyle appears. Reggie takes off on the run, turning the corner and starting down the stairs. She passes the same sleeping man in the lobby, exits the hotel.

EXT. HOTEL ENTRANCE—NIGHT

Reggie approaches a waiting taxi. Speaking loudly in French, she opens and closes the door without getting inside, hands the driver some money and waves him off

INT. HOTEL LOBBY—NIGHT

It is deserted, except for the sleeping Night Porter, as REGGIE comes running down the stairs.

EXT. HOTEL ENTRANCE—NIGHT

Dyle emerges from the hotel, approaches another taxi.

DYLE

(pointing)

Follow that taxi!

Dyle gets inside. As the taxi pulls away. Reggie, who was hiding in the shadows, stands up and reveals herself. She watches Dyle's taxi pull away.

EXT. LES HALLES—NIGHT

Reggie and Bartholomew walking. The Central Market is teeming with activity—trucks creeping around other trucks, cases of fruit and vegetables stacked on every inch of sidewalk, workers of all types milling around, unloading trucks and stacking crates, little electric carts scooting in and out—and nearby, one of the huge, high-roofed sheds where the butchers work.

Two shot—Reggie and Bartholomew, camera leading them as they walk.

BARTHOLOMEW

Were you followed?

REGGIE

Yes, by Dyle, but I lost him. I'm beginning to think women make the best spies.

BARTHOLOMEW

Agents.

REGGIE

He has a gun, Mr. Bartholomew.

BARTHOLOMEW

No.

REGGIE

But I saw it.

BARTHOLOMEW

No, that's not Carson Dyle.

REGGIE

Carson?

BARTHOLOMEW

There's only one Dyle connected with this affair, Mrs. Lampert, that's Carson Dyle.

REGGIE

You mean you've known about him all along?

Bartholomew looks at her for a moment, then glances around; his attention is drawn inside the doorway.

INT. LES HALLES BUTCHERS' SHED—NIGHT

Almost as far as the eye can see, row upon row of beef sides, hung on hooks.

Two shot—Reggie and Bartholomew (traveling) as Reggie looks at the hanging beef.

BARTHOLOMEW

It's enough to make you a vegetarian, isn't it?

REGGIE

It's just lucky that I'm not heading next to one of those things right now. Why didn't you tell me you knew about Dyle?

BARTHOLOMEW

I didn't see any point, Dyle is dead.

REGGIE

(stops to face Bartholomew)

Mr. Bartholomew, what is all this about?

INT. LES HALLES BISTRO—NIGHT

Close shot—Bartholomew, leaning in.

BARTHOLOMEW

In 1944, five members of the OSS, the Military Espionage Unit, were ordered behind the German lines for the purpose of delivering $250,000 in gold to the French Underground.

Close shot—Reggie, listening.

BARTHOLOMEW

The five men were, of course, were your husband, Charles, the three men who showed up at his funeral yesterday, and Carson Dyle.

REGGIE

Oh!

BARTHOLOMEW

Instead of delivering the gold, they stole it.

REGGIE

How?

BARTHOLOMEW

By burying it, then reporting the Germans had captured it. All they had to do was come back after the war, dig it up and split it five ways. Quarter of a million dollars with no questions asked.

REGGIE

May I have a cigarette, please?

BARTHOLOMEW pulls out a package and she takes one, looks at it and rips off the filter tip. He winces.

REGGIE

I can't stand those things. It's like drinking coffee through a veil.

BARTHOLOMEW

Everything went smoothly enough until after the gold was buried. Then before they could get out, they were ambushed by a German patrol. A machine gun separated Scobie from his right hand and caught Carson Dyle full in the stomach . . .

Reggie takes the cigarette out of her mouth, puts it down and takes another.

What was wrong with that one?

REGGIE

Nothing, I guess. What happened then?

BARTHOLOMEW

Have you any idea what these things cost over here?

REGGIE

Please go on, Mr. Bartholomew—what happened then?

BARTHOLOMEW

Carson Dyle was dead, but Scobie was able to travel.

Bartholomew stops talking as a waiter approaches the table.

WAITER

La soupe, c'est pour qui?

REGGIE

Pour moi.

BARTHOLOMEW

(sighs)

Where was I?

REGGIE

Carson Dyle was dead.

BARTHOLOMEW

Yes, Carson Dyle was dead. The others finally got back to the base and waited for the war to end. Only Charles couldn't wait quite as long as the others. He beat them back to the gold, took everything for himself and disappeared. It's taken Gideon, Tex, and Scobie all this time to catch up with him again.

REGGIE

But if they stole all that money, why can't you arrest them?

BARTHOLOMEW

(puts his finger to his lips and shushes her)

We know what happened from the bits and pieces we were able to paste together. We still have no proof.

REGGIE

What's this got to do with the CIO?

BARTHOLOMEW

CIA, Mrs. Lampert. It's an extension of the wartime OSS. It's our money and we want it back.

REGGIE

I'm sorry Mr. Bartholomew, but nothing you've said has changed my mind. I'm leaving Paris tonight.

BARTHOLOMEW

I wouldn't advise that Mrs. Lampert, better consider what happened to your husband when he tried to leave. Those men won't be very far away no matter where you go. In fact, I don't even see any point in your changing hotels. Now please help us, Mrs. Lampert. Your government is counting on you.

REGGIE

(sighs)

I suppose if I'm going to die, I might as well do it for my country.

BARTHOLOMEW

That's the spirit. Here's what I want you to do. We're anxious to know who this man is, the one calling himself Dyle. I want you to find out.

REGGIE

Why me?

BARTHOLOMEW

You're in an ideal position. He trusts you.

(grinning)

Besides, you yourself said women make the best spies.

REGGIE

Agents.

EXT. HOTEL (PLACE ST. ANDRÉ DES ARTS)—LATE AFTERNOON

Dyle leaves the hotel with Reggie watching from a window behind him. Dyle starts walking and passes a woman cleaning a window railing, snapping her rag against it. The dust gets into his eyes and he pauses, just as Reggie is leaving, following him. She almost bumps into him and immediately runs back inside.

EXT. PLACE ST. ANDRÉ DES ARTS—LATE AFTERNOON

Dyle passes a sidewalk cafe on the corner, then a girl painting, her easel set up in the middle of the sidewalk. He stops to turns to look at her work. He almost spots Reggie, who's following him. At the last second she spins around and sits at the sidewalk cafe's nearest table, her back to DYLE. It is already occupied by a middle-aged tourist.

Two shot—Reggie and tourist, complete with camera, beret and guide book, looks up from his coffee, surprised. He grins at Reggie, surprised to find such a beautiful woman suddenly sharing his table. She smiles back.

Reggie turns around to look for Dyle and sees he's moving on from the painter. She gets up to follow and the tourist runs after her.

TOURIST

Fraulein? Fraulein!

REGGIE

(shouting at the tourist)

What are you doing following me? It's gonna look like a parade! Stop it!

Dyle steps into the street and is cut off by a car, turning the corner. Reggie is once again in his line of sight so she turns and grabs the tourist by the elbow, walking away from Dyle.

REGGIE

(to the tourist, in a familiar way)

How are you? How nice to see you. When did you arrive? It's a lovely time to stay. Are you having a good time? So many things to see.

Reggie sits back down with the tourist. She looks back and sees Dyle is now crossing the street. She gets up and runs after him. The tourist gets up and tries to follow her, again.

TOURIST

Fraulein! Fraulein!

REGGIE

(to the tourist)

If you don't stop following me, I'll call the police!

She sees Dyle jump onto a moving street car.

REGGIE

Taxi!

Dyle speeds away as Reggie jumps into a taxi.

INT. AMERICAN EXPRESS—LATE AFTERNOON

Dyle enters and immediately goes to a stairway leading down. Reggie enters just as he disappears from the frame and follows him downstairs. A sign indicates it leads to the *MAIL ROOM & TELEPHONES.*

INT. AMERICAN EXPRESS MAIL ROOM—
LATE AFTERNOON

Dyle walks to one of several windows. A sign over it reading: "A–D."

Med. shot—Reggie comes down the stairs. Suddenly she stops.

Med. shot—Dyle. Camera zooms in to sign on *D*.

Close shot—Reggie, a confused look on her face.

Med. shot—Dyle as his turn comes, he addresses the Clerk

DYLE

Dyle, please. D-Y-L-E.

CLERK

Yes, Mr. Dyle. I remember.

Close shot—Reggie, watching.

Med. shot—mail window. The clerk takes out a bundle of letters and quickly sorts through it.

CLERK

No, I'm sorry Mr. Dyle, nothing today.

DYLE

Thank you.

He turns and starts to leave.

VOICE (O.S.)

(over the loudspeaker)

Mr. Dyle, please, you're wanted on the telephone. Mr. Dyle, cabin four. Mr. Dyle phone booth four, please.

He stops and comes down the stairs, going to the back of the room and into the cabin marked *4*.

Camera dollies to discover Reggie two cabins away, on the phone.

INT. DYLE'S CABIN

DYLE

(on the phone)

Yes.

REGGIE (V.O.)

(whispering)

Good morning, Mr. Dyle.

DYLE

(smiles)

Reggie?

INT. REGGIE'S CABIN

REGGIE

It's the only name I've got. How about you?

INT. DYLE'S CABIN

DYLE

I know cat and mouse. You've got me. What do you want to know?

REGGIE (V.O.)

Why you lied to me?

DYLE

I had to. That's all I knew you were in on the whole thing.

INT. REGGIE'S CABIN

REGGIE

I'm trying to find out who you are.

DYLE

But you know my name is Dyle.

INT. REGGIE'S CABIN

REGGIE

Carson Dyle is *dead.*

INT. DYLE'S CABIN

DYLE

Yes, he is. He was my brother.

INT. REGGIE'S CABIN

REGGIE

Your brother.

INT. DYLE'S CABIN

DYLE

The Army thinks he was killed in action by the Germans, but I think they did it—Tex, Gideon, Scobie, and your husband, because my brother wouldn't go along with their scheme to steal the gold. I think he threatened to turn them in and they killed him. And I'm trying to prove it. They think I'm working with them, but I'm not, Reggie. I'm on your side. Just believe that.

REGGIE

How can I, you lie to me, just the way Charles did. After promising you wouldn't. Oh, I want to believe you, Peter. Oh, I can't call you that anymore, can I? Take me a while to get used to your new name? What is it?

(pauses)

Hmm? Hello? Hello?

She hangs up the phone, opens the door of the cabin and steps out.

Med. shot—Reggie steps out of her cabin and walks over to Dyle's. It's empty, the receiver hanging by its cord.

INT. AMERICAN EXPRESS—DAY

Dyle and Scobie stand together, waiting for the elevator, Scobie clearly holding a gun in the pocket of his raincoat.

SCOBIE

Do anything funny or try to talk to anyone and I'll kill you Dyle.

DYLE

You'll wreck your raincoat.

The elevator doors open, Dyle and Scobie enter. A middle aged woman tries to come in after them.

SCOBIE

Take the next car, please.

Scobie gestures with his metal hand. The woman looks at it and steps away. Dyle and Scobie stare at each other silently as the elevator climbs to the top floor.

INT. TOP FLOOR LANDING—LATE AFTERNOON

Scobie follows Dyle out of the elevator. Dyle looks back at Scobie who is nearly too tall to go through without bending down.

DYLE

Look out, didn't want you to bump your head.

SCOBIE

Alright, get in there.

INT—STAIRWELL—LATE AFTERNOON

Through the door, which Scobie closes behind them, is a flight of stairs, leading up to a second floor.

SCOBIE

Alright, turn around.

Dyle turns to find Scobie's gun out of the pocket and pointing at him. Scobie now transfers it to his metal hand and goes to DYLE, where he proceeds to frisk him.

Finding the gun Dyle carries in his inside coat pocket, Scobie removes it. During the following conversation he will shake open the revolving magazine and let the bullets fall out onto the floor before handing back the emptied gun to Dyle. Then he will transfer his own gun back to his good hand.

SCOBIE

Now, sit down.

Shrugging, Dyle sits on the third step.

DYLE

Now what?

SCOBIE

We wait with our mouth shut.

Dyle yawns wide.

DYLE

I am sorry about that.

INT. AMERICAN EXPRESS—NIGHT

The last employees leave the building as the watchman locks the front door after them.

INT. TOP FLOOR LANDING—NIGHT

In the semi-darkness, Dyle is still sitting on the third step, SCOBIE still facing him with a gun.

SCOBIE

Okay, up there.

Dyle gets to his feet and starts up the stairs, followed by Scobie. Dyle stops at the door.

DYLE

Do I knock or something?

SCOBIE

Open it. Keep right on going.

Dyle opens the door. The stairs continue up.

DYLE

The view. It better be worth it.

EXT. AMERICAN EXPRESS—ROOFTOP—NIGHT

A spectacular view of the Paris rooftops and the city lights beyond. Dyle and Scobie come out onto a level portion of roof, behind a large neon sign. Dyle puts on his glasses, turns around and briefly checks out the view.

DYLE

Very pretty. Now what?

Scobie lowers his gun at Dyle.

DYLE

I was afraid of that.

Scobie starts advancing toward Dyle, toward the edge of the roof

SCOBIE

I will give you a chance Dyle, which is more than you'd give me. Where's the money?

DYLE

Is that why you dragged me all the way up here to ask me that? She has it.

SCOBIE

And I say maybe you both have it. One. More. Time, Dyle—where is it?

DYLE

Supposing I had it, which I don't, do you really think I just hand it over to you?

SCOBIE

Step back.

DYLE

(looks over the edge of the roof)

Back where?

SCOBIE

(whispers)

That's the idea.

DYLE

No, no, just a minute. Take it easy . . .

Scobie starts walking toward him. Moving quickly, Dyle lashes out and grabs Scobie's gun hand, lifting it upward. The gun fires.

Following through, Dyle punches the large man full in the jaw, sending him reeling. Scobie drops the gun and it skids across the edge of the roof. Both men lunge for it.

Scobie turns toward Dyle, overpowers him, and menaces him with his metal hand. Scobie and Dyle move across the roof in a clench, Scobie lifting Dyle into the air back toward the edge of the roof.

Working his arms between their two bodies, Dyle suddenly flails them out and the hold is broken. As Scobie stumbles away his metal claw rips through Dyle's coat and the flesh on his back, a wound extending from Dyle's spine to his shoulder.

Dyle falls to his knees in agony, nearly off the edge of the roof. Scobie comes after him and falls into the neon sign, raising sparks. He again overpowers Dyle, who's on the ground, and menaces him with his claw while Dyle struggles to keep it away from his face.

Dyle manages to throw Scobie over his head; Scobie tumbles and Dyle grabs his claw arm again before Scobie throws him into a wall. Dyle climbs up a ladder then leaps off it into Scobie and the two grapple til Scobie pushes Dyle over the side of the sloped roof but he manages to grab onto the edge.

Scobie moves slowly toward him, clearly feeling the effects of the brutal fight. He goes to kick Dyle in the head, sending him seven stories down to the sidewalk, but Dyle grabs his ankle one-handed, flips him onto his back and scrambles up after him.

The two men get to their feet and face off. Dyle runs back and forth as Scobie swipes at him with his metal hand, three times. On the last swipe Dyle falls to the ground near the edge of the roof and Scobie trips over him, falling over the side of the roof, screaming. Scobie beats wildly at the the slate with his claw as he slides down the slope.

Close shot—roof edge. There appears to be no sign of Scobie.

Close shot—Dyle looking over the edge of the roof.

DYLE

Herman?

Close shot—Scobie hanging by his claw.

SCOBIE

What?

DYLE

(chuckles)

How're you doing?

SCOBIE

How do you think?

DYLE

If you get bored, try riding "love thine neighbor" a hundred times on the side of the building.

Med. shot—Scobie as he hangs, seven stories over the street, by his metal hand.

INT. HOTEL CORRIDOR—THIRD LANDING—NIGHT

A tired, wounded Dyle exits the elevator and goes to enter his room. The hotel manager is next door, busy taping a piece of cardboard over the hole ripped in Reggie's door by Scobie's metal hand the night before. Dyle leaves the elevator and goes to his own door.

MANAGER

Monsieur, next time please, use the keyhole.

INT. REGGIE'S ROOM—NIGHT

Reggie, lying awake in bed, sits up when she hears Dyle moving about in his room. She goes to the connecting door.

REGGIE

Is that you?

BRIAN

Yeah.

She unlocks her side, tries the knob, finds it still bolted from his side. Dyle opens the door with his torn, bloody jacket in his hand.

REGGIE

Didn't anyone ever tell you it's impolite to—

(seeing the jacket and his injured back)

What happened?

DYLE

Oh, I met a man with sharp nails.

REGGIE

Scobie?

DYLE

I left him hanging around the American Express.

REGGIE

Come on—I've got something that stings like crazy.

She goes toward the bathroom with Dyle following her into her room.

DYLE

Now you're the kind of girl that would have something like that.

REGGIE

Sit down.

She returns with a bottle of disinfectant and gauze. Dyle goes to grab a chair and looks at the bottle.

DYLE

Wait a minute—what is this stuff?

REGGIE

(pouring it into a wad of gauze)

Marvelous stuff, gonna hurt you much more than it's going hurt me.

DYLE

(sits down, facing away from her)

I bet.

Reggie tears a larger hole in his shirt so she can attend to his wound.

DYLE

Did you hear something rip?

REGGIE

No.

DYLE

Oh, that's odd . . .

Reggie applies the disinfectant.

DYLE

Ouch! Listen, I only came in for an estimate.

REGGIE

Sit still. It's not too bad. You won't be able to lie on your back for a few days, but then you can lie from any position, can't you? Does it hurt?

DYLE

(laughs sarcastically)

Oh, oh!

REGGIE

Does it hurt?

DYLE

Are you kidding? Have you got a bullet I can bite, like they do in the movies?

REGGIE

Are you really Carson Dyle's brother?

DYLE

Well, if you'd like to see my passport . . .

REGGIE

Passport? What kind of a proof is that?

DYLE

Well, would you like to see where I was tattooed?

REGGIE

Yes.

DYLE

Alright, we'll drive around that way.

(whimpers as she applies more disinfectant)

REGGIE

You could at least tell me what your first name is, these days.

DYLE

Alexander.

REGGIE

Okay, Alexander. You're done.

DYLE

(stands up)

Good.

REGGIE

You are a new man.

DYLE

I'm sorry the old one couldn't tell you the truth, but I had to find out your part in all this.

Dyle goes back to his room, out of the frame. Reggie sits down in the same chair.

REGGIE

Is there a Mrs. Dyle?

DYLE (O.S.)

Yes, but we're divorced.

REGGIE

I thought that was Peter Joshua.

DYLE (O.S.)

I'm just as difficult to live with as he was.

REGGIE

Alex, how can you tell if anyone's lying or not?

Dyle reenters Reggie's room, putting on a new shirt.

DYLE

You can't.

REGGIE

There must be some way.

DYLE

No, no. There's an old riddle about two tribes of Indians: The white feet always tell the truth and the black feet always lie. So one day you meet an Indian, you say, hey Indian —what are you a truthful white foot or lying black foot? He says I'm a truthful white foot, but which is he?

REGGIE

Well, why couldn't you just look at his feet?

DYLE

Because he's wearing moccasins.

REGGIE

Well then he's a truthful white foot, of course.

DYLE

But why not a lying black foot?

REGGIE

Which one are you?

DYLE

A truthful white foot.

REGGIE

Come in. Sit down.

DYLE

(sits)

Right, you wanna look at my feet?

REGGIE

(sitting on his lap)

Yes.

DYLE

Hey, knock it off now. Come on, Reggie, listen to me.

REGGIE

Oh, here it comes, the fatherly talk. You forget I'm already a widow.

DYLE

So was Juliet at fifteen.

REGGIE

I'm not fifteen.

DYLE

Well, that's your trouble. You're too old for me.

REGGIE

Can't you be serious?

DYLE

Oh, you just had a horrible word.

REGGIE

What did I say?

DYLE

Serious. When a man gets to be my age, that's the last word he ever wants to hear. I don't wanna be serious, and I especially don't want you to be.

REGGIE

Okay, well just sit around all day long being frivolous. How about that?

She starts kissing him.

DYLE

Reggie, cut it out.

REGGIE

(stopping)

Okay.

DYLE

Well now what are you doing?

REGGIE

Cutting it out.

DYLE

Who told you to do that?

REGGIE

You did.

DYLE

Oh, I'm not through complaining yet.

REGGIE

Oh.

She starts kissing him again.

DYLE

Now cut it out.

REGGIE

Alex, I think I love you.

She kisses him on the mouth, he gives in. The phone rings and he tries to talk as she continues kissing him.

DYLE

Hey, the telephone is ringing.

REGGIE

Never mind whoever it is won't give up, and neither will I.

DYLE

Go ahead, take it.

The phone continues to ring and she continues to kiss him.

Finally, Reggie reaches out to the bedstand and takes the phone off the hook. She brings the receiver up to their mouths and mumbles into it.

REGGIE

(on phone)

Hello, I'm sorry. Uh, I was just nibbling on something.

INT. TEX'S ROOM—NIGHT

Tex is lying in bed, speaking into the phone. Gideon is standing beside him.

TEX

(on the phone)

See, I'd appreciate it mighty highly if you'd, uh, wiggle on over the room 46 and chew the fat for a spell.

INT. REGGIE'S ROOM—NIGHT

Dyle is watching her.

REGGIE

(on the phone)

Could you give me one good reason why I should?

INT. TEX'S ROOM—NIGHT

TEX

(on the phone)

Yeah, a little one, about six or seven, keeps calling for Aunt Reggie. Ain't that cute?

INT. REGGIE'S ROOM—NIGHT

She covers the phone and turns to Dyle in alarm.

REGGIE

They've got Jean-Louis!

(into the phone)

I'll be right there.

INT. TEX'S ROOM—NIGHT

Close shot—Jean-Louis on Scobie's knee, the large man holding him with his good hand, the metal one in his pocket.

Wider shot—Tex sits next to them while Gideon nervously paces the floor. When Gideon begins sneezing he takes the small bottle of pills from his pocket and downs one or two, swallowing some water.

SCOBIE

Hey Tex. Do something with this kid, will you? My whole leg's going sleep.

Tex lifts Jean-Louis and puts him atop a bureau next to him.

TEX

Upsy-daisy.

JEAN-LOUIS

Are you a real cowboy?

TEX

Yes. Sure I am, kid.

JEAN-LOUIS

So where's your gun?

Tex takes out his gun and twirls it for him.

GIDEON

Will you put that thing away?!

A knock at the door. Gideon goes to open it and Reggie and Dyle enter. She sees Jean-Louis and Tex's gun.

REGGIE

Jean-Louis!

TEX

Howdy, Mrs. Lampert.

SCOBIE

(standing up)

So who invited him?

BRIAN

Well Herman, I can see you had a happy landing.

REGGIE

I must call Sylvie right away.

Gideon closes the door behind her.

GIDEON

I'm afraid that'll have to wait, Mrs. Lampert.

REGGIE

But it's his mother!

GIDEON

She won't be anybody's mother unless you answer some questions.

TEX

This ain't no game Mrs. Lampert

SCOBIE

I want that money now!

DYLE

Why don't you keep quiet and stop threatening the child? He hasn't got the money and neither has Mrs. Lampert

The three men look at him, surprised by his tone.

SCOBIE

Then who does?

DYLE

I don't know, Herman. Maybe you do.

Camera switches to Scobie as Dyle identifies him.

SCOBIE

Me?

DYLE

(looking at Tex)

Or you.

TEX

Oh, come on.

BRIAN

(looking at Gideon)

Or him.

GIDEON

Oh, that's the most ridiculous thing.

SCOBIE

(dismissively)

Listen to this man.

TEX

The man has gone loco.

DYLE

Now hold it—suppose one of you found Charles here in Paris. He even bumped into him by accident. Followed him when he tried to run out again. Cornered him on the train, threw him out the window without bothering to tell the other two, took all the money for yourself.

SCOBIE

If one of us did that, he wouldn't hang around here waiting for the other two to figure it out.

DYLE

But he'd have to. Don't you see? If he'd left, he'd be admitting his guilt. Whoever it is has to wait here pretending to look for the money, waiting for the rest of us to give up and go home.

SCOBIE

(to the other three men)

He's just trying to throw us off. They got it, I tell you.

TEX

Why don't we search their rooms?

DYLE

(pauses, looks at Reggie)

That's all right with us.

TEX

(moving towards the door)

Well then what are we wasting time for? Let's go.

DYLE

While we're waiting, we'll search yours.

SCOBIE

Not my room!

DYLE

Well Herman, you have something to hide?

(a pause, then smiling)

Then there are no objections. Alright, here's my key.

Dyle holds up his key.

SCOBIE

I'll take that.

Scobie takes it and walks past him, out the door. Gideon follows.

REGGIE

My room is open.

TEX

(as he walks out the door behind the others)

Now you two just make yourselves to home here.

DYLE

Well, let's get busy.

He lifts Jean-Louis from the bureau and puts him down on the bed.

DYLE

Come on, Jean-Louis, come on. Oh, that's fine.

(talking to Reggie)

Who gets your vote?

REGGIE

Scobie. He's the one who objected.

DYLE

(handing her the boy)

Alright, I'll take Tex's room and Gideon's. You take Jean-Louis with you and bolt the door from inside.

REGGIE

Come on, Jean-Louis, we'll have a treasure hunt. Okay?

She takes Jean-Louis' hand and leaves.

DYLE

(ushering them out the door)

Come on.

INT. REGGIE'S ROOM—NIGHT

Close shot—airlines bag. Camera pulls back to include Gideon, unzipping it as it lies on the table in the center of the room. Tex is behind him, going through a drawer.

GIDEON

Tex?

Gideon dumps the contents out onto the table. The two men start rifling through it.

TEX

Man, it's Charlie's stuff!

GIDEON

Looks like it.

TEX

We've got to call Herman.

GIDEON

What for? If it's not here, why bother him?

TEX

And if it is?

GIDEON

Why bother him?

TEX

(laughs)

Alright. So there's nothing missing.

GIDEON

No, everything's here. The police have kindly provided us with a list.

TEX

(taking the list from Gideon)

Sure ain't nothing here worth no quarter of a million dollars.

GIDEON

Not unless we're blind.

(walks away towards the closet)

I keep telling myself we've stolen a great deal of money, but up to now I've yet to see a penny of it.

TEX

You think maybe we're fishing up the wrong stream?

GIDEON

Meaning what?

TEX

Suppose one of us has it, you know, like the man says. Now that'd be mighty distasteful. Us bein' veterans of the same war and all.

Two shot—the men face each other at a close distance.

GIDEON

Well, you know, I'd tell you if I had it.

TEX

Oh, naturally, just like I'd tell you if I had it.

GIDEON

Naturally. And that goes for Herman too.

TEX AND GIDEON

Naturally.

The two men look at one another, then smile—then laugh.

INT. SCOBIE'S ROOM—NIGHT

Reggie on the phone, sitting up in bed. Jean-Louis is in her lap.

REGGIE

He's all right Sylvie, honestly, just hurry over as soon as you can. Okay, goodbye. Now, if you had a treasure, where would you hide it?

JEAN-LOUIS

I would bury it in the garden.

REGGIE

Well, swear that this man doesn't have a garden.

JEAN-LOUIS

Oh, neither do I.

REGGIE

You don't? Well, if you had to hide it in this room, where would you put it?

JEAN-LOUIS

Up there.

Reggie looks to where Jean-Louis is pointing—to the top of the high armoire.

REGGIE

On top of that cupboard? You know something? You may be right.

Taking one of the straight chairs to the armoire, she stands on it. Although she is still not high enough to see anything, by standing on tip-toes she is able to reach with her hand over the top and grope around blindly.

REGGIE

Oh, I hope I don't find any hairy little things living up here. Hey, there is something, and it's heavy!

Reggie has finally managed to pull down the case—a rectangular black bag about the size and shape of a trombone case. She climbs off the chair.

JEAN-LOUIS

I found it! I found it! I found it! I found it!

REGGIE

If you think you're getting credit for this, you're crazy.

Jean-Louis runs out the door.

INT. HOTEL CORRIDOR—THIRD LANDING—NIGHT

Jean-Louis runs down the hall.

JEAN-LOUIS

We won! We won! We won! We won! We won! We won! We won! We won! We found it! We found it!

Overhead shot as the three men come out of the rooms they were searching. They run past Jean-Louis and squeeze together into Scobie's room.

INT. SCOBIE'S ROOM—NIGHT

As Dyle, Tex and Gideon enter, Reggie is placing the little straight black chair to its original position. There is no sign of the black case.

DYLE

Did you find it?

REGGIE

No.

GIDEON

What do you mean no?

TEX

The kid was yelling there.

JEAN-LOUIS

(pointing atop the armoire)

Up there! It's up there!

REGGIE

Believe me, there's nothing up there.

Tex grabs the chair and moves it to the armoire, climbing up on it and grabbing the bag. He climbs back down and brings it to the table, looking at it greedily. He unclasps and opens it.

Close shot—inside the case, neatly packed in velvet fittings, is a metal artificial hand.

TEX

Oh, jumping frijoles, it's Herman's spare.

Camera switches to a disappointed Gideon then Dyle. Slowly Tex lowers the lid. The men avoid looking at one another.

REGGIE

Where is he?

DYLE

He's over in my room.

The men look at one another and head out of the room, Dyle first.

INT. DYLE'S ROOM—NIGHT

Dyle enters the room with the others behind him. The sound of running water can be heard coming from behind the closed door to the bathroom and Dyle is the first to notice water leaking out from under the door.

DYLE

You'd better take the boy out in the hall.

INT. BATHROOM—NIGHT

Dyle opens the door with Tex and Gideon crowding behind them.

Close shot—Scobie, still dressed in his raincoat, lies face up, his head submerged in the filled tub, the water now pouring over the edge. His face is distorted. Dyle's hand appears and turns off the water.

TEX

Oh, now who would've done a mean thing like that?

DYLE

(looking carefully at both)

I'm not quite sure.

TEX

Well, this ain't my room.

GIDEON

Mine neither.

DYLE

(walking between them)

Oh, the police aren't going to like this a bit.

GIDEON

(looking at the body)

We could dry him off and take him down the hall to his own room, he really doesn't look too bad.

TEX

Oh, poor old Herman. Seems like him and good luck always was strangers. Well maybe now he'll meet up with his other hand someplace.

INT. SCOBIE'S ROOM—DAY

Close shot of a smiling maid entering the room. Her eyes widen at the realization that the man is dead. Then she screams.

Zoom in close to Scobie, lying in bed with the covers up around his chin. His eyes are open but lifeless.

GRANDPIERRE (V.O.)

A man drowned in his bed. Impossible.

INT. GRANDPIERRE'S OFFICE—LATE AFTERNOON

Close shot—Grandpierre at his desk.

GRANDPIERRE

And in his pajamas—the second one, in his pajamas. So it was stupid. Stop lying to me.

Reverse shot—Grandpierre is talking to (left to right) Dyle, Reggie, Tex, and Gideon.

GRANDPIERRE

This nose tells me when you are lying. It is never mistaken, not in 23 years.

(tapping the side of his nose)

This nose will make me commissaire of police.

GRANDPIERRE (S.O.)

Mr. Dyle or Mr. Joshua, which is it?

DYLE

Dyle.

GRANDPIERRE

And yet you werere registered in Megev as Mr. Joshua. Didn't you know it was against the law to register under an assumed name?

DYLE

No, I didn't.

REGGIE

It's done in America all the time.

Grandpierre raps for silence on his desk.

GRANDPIERRE

None of you will be permitted to leave Paris until this matter is cleared up. Only I warn you, I will be watching. We use the guillotine in this country. I have always suspected that the blade coming down causes no more than a slight tickling sensation on the back of the neck. It is only a guess, of course. I hope none of you ever finds out for certain.

GIDEON

[*Sneezes*]

EXT. QUAI MONTEBELLO—LATE AFTERNOON

Reggie and Dyle walking along the quai, next to the Seine, camera leading.

REGGIE

Who do you think did it? Gideon?

DYLE

Possibly.

REGGIE

Or Tex?

DYLE

Possibly.

REGGIE

You are a fat lot of help.

DYLE

That's right.

REGGIE

Can I have one of those?

DYLE

One of what?

They have passed an ice-cream wagon on the corner of the Pont au Double. Dyle shrugs and they double back.

REGGIE

I think Tex did it.

BRIAN

Oh.

REGGIE

(to the vendor)

Vanille et chocolat s'il vous plait.

During the following, the vendor makes a double-decker cone and hands it to Reggie. Dyle pays and they resume their walk—all with no break in the dialogue.

DYLE

Why do you think Tex did it?

REGGIE

Because I really suspect Gideon and it's always the person you don't suspect.

DYLE

Do women think it's feminine to be so illogical or can't they help it?

REGGIE

What's so illogical about that?

DYLE

Well, you just said that it's always the one you don't suspect, and you suspect Gideon, so therefore it must be Tex. But on the other hand, if you suspect Tex, it must be the other fellow Gideon—hahaha.

REGGIE

I guess I just can't help it.

DYLE

Hmm? Who?

REGGIE

Women.

DYLE

Oh.

REGGIE

You know, I can't help feeling rather sorry for Scobie. Wouldn't it be nice if we were like that?

DYLE

What? Like Scobie?

REGGIE

No. Gene Kelly. You remember when he danced down here by the river? An American in Paris without a care in the world?

DYLE

Hmm.

REGGIE

You know, this is good, want some?

She offers him her cone, thrusting it forward with enough force to dislodge the ice-cream. It lands right next to his lapel, over his outside breast pocket.

DYLE

No, thanks.

REGGIE

Oh!

DYLE

And I guess you don't, don't you?

He pulls open the pocket with two sticky fingers and looks inside, then shakes his head sadly at what he sees. Reggie still holds the empty cone, not knowing what to do with it. Seeing this, he takes it, tosses it into the river and licks his fingers.

REGGIE

I'm sorry. Alex, I'm scared.

DYLE

Yes, I know.

REGGIE

I can't think of any reason why he was killed.

DYLE

Well, perhaps someone thought the four shares were too many.

REGGIE

What makes you think that this someone is gonna be satisfied with three? He wants it all, Alex. That means we are in his way too.

DYLE

That's right.

REGGIE

We've got to do something. I mean, in any minute now, we could be assassinated. Would you do anything like that?

DYLE

What, assassinate someone?

REGGIE

No, swing down from there on a rope to save the woman you love. Like the Hunchback of Notre Dame.

Another angle including the Cathedral of Notre Dame in the background.

DYLE

Oh, who put that there?

INT. HOTEL CORRIDOR—THIRD LANDING—LATE AFTERNOON

As Reggie and Dyle step from the elevator.

REGGIE

Hurry up and change. I'm starved.

DYLE

Let me know what you wanna reach so that I can pick out a suit that matches. Hahahaha.

He goes into his room and she goes into hers.

INT. REGGIE'S ROOM—LATE AFTERNOON

She enters, fixes her hair in the mirror, then goes to the door connecting her room with Dyle's. She unlocks it, tries to open it, but finds it locked. Disappointed, she knocks.

INT. DYLE'S ROOM—LATE AFTERNOON

He calls to her through the closed door as he empties his pockets.

DYLE

What do you want?

REGGIE (O.S.)

It's the house detective, why don't you have a girl in there?

DYLE

God, you're a pest.

REGGIE (O.S.)

Can I come in?

DYLE

No, I'm gonna take a bath!

INT. REGGIE'S ROOM—LATE AFTERNOON

REGGIE

Oh, wouldn't it be better if you did it in here?

DYLE (O.S.)

What for?

REGGIE

Well, I wouldn't wanna use that tub. And anyway, I don't wanna be alone, I'm afraid.

INT. DYLE'S ROOM—LATE AFTERNOON

DYLE

You're only next door, if anything happens, holler.

REGGIE

[*Screams*]

INT. DYLE'S ROOM—LATE AFTERNOON

Dyle races for the connecting door, pulls back the bolt and rushes in.

INT. REGGIE'S ROOM—LATE AFTERNOON

As Dyle enters.

DYLE

Reggie?

He wheels as the door is slammed and Reggie, who had been standing behind it, locks it and pockets the key.

REGGIE

Got you. Ha ha!

DYLE

Did you ever hear the story of the boy who cried a wolf?

REGGIE

The shower is in there.

DYLE

Oh, come on, Reggie, open the door.

REGGIE

This is a ludicrous situation—I can think of a dozen men who just longing to use my shower.

DYLE

Why don't you call one of them?

REGGIE

I dare you.

DYLE

Oh, you're a nut.

Dyle looks at her, then sits down and starts to remove his shoes.

REGGIE

What are you doing?

DYLE

I'm taking off my shoes. What do you think I'm doing? Did you ever hear of anyone taking a shower with their shoes on?

Shoes off, Dyle starts for the bathroom, humming.

DYLE

I usually sing a medley of old favorites when I'm in the shower. Oh, any requests?

REGGIE

Shut the door.

BRIAN

(from the bathroom doorway)

Oh, I'm afraid I don't know that one, Miss. Oh well . . .

REGGIE

Shut the door!

INT. BATHROOM—LATE AFTERNOON

Med. shot—Dyle turns on the shower and steps in, fully clothed. He turns around, making sure his suit gets uniformly soaked.

DYLE

Why? Come in and watch. Drip dry!

He takes the soap and begins washing as if he were washing himself without the suit.

REGGIE

(amused)

How often do you go through this little ritual?

DYLE

Oh, every day, the manufacturer recommends it.

REGGIE

I don't believe it.

DYLE

Oh yes, it's written on it.

He opens his coat, removes his glasses, puts them on and reads a label inside his lapel.

DYLE

Look at the small print: "*Wear this suit during washing help protect its shape.*"

He lifts his hand and starts scrubbing at his watchband.

DYLE

Waterproof. Acro-nylon. Triforce-resistant. Plastic. Rust-proof. Flyproof. Proof-proof.

REGGIE

(laughing)

You're the nut.

DYLE

Nut-proof...

INT. REGGIE'S ROOM—LATE AFTERNOON

Reggie closes the door, laughing. The phone rings and she answers it.

REGGIE

Yes?

INT. BARTHOLOMEW'S APARTMENT—LATE AFTERNOON

Bartholomew is bouncing up and down on his knees, some kind of exercise. He continues as they speak.

BARTHOLOMEW

(on the phone)

Mrs. Lampert, Bartholomew. I spoke to Washington, Mrs. Lampert.

INT. REGGIE'S ROOM—LATE AFTERNOON

REGGIE

(on the phone)

Go ahead Mr. Bartholomew, I'm listening.

BARTHOLOMEW

(stops bouncing)

Uh, well, I uh, told them what you said about this man being Carson Dyle's brother. I asked them what they knew about it, and they told me. You're not gonna like this, Mrs. Lampert—Carson Dyle had no brother. Mrs. Lampert?

INT. REGGIE'S ROOM—LATE AFTERNOON

Close shot—REGGIE on the phone, looking like the rug has been pulled out from under her.

REGGIE

Are you sure there's no mistake?

INT. BARTHOLOMEW'S APARTMENT—LATE AFTERNOON

BARTHOLOMEW

None whatsoever. Please be careful, Mrs. Lampert. Bye.

INT. REGGIE'S ROOM—LATE AFTERNOON

Reggie slowly lowers the phone to its cradle, a worried expression on her face. Then the bathroom door opens and Dyle appears in a bathrobe.

DYLE

I left all my drip-dried dripping. Is that all right?

(pauses)

What's the matter? Is something wrong?

She shakes her head.

DYLE

Oh, you're probably weak from hunger, you've only eaten five times today. I'll get someone to fix up my suit quickly and take you out to dinner.

REGGIE

(downcast)

Let's go somewhere crowded. I feel like a lot of people.

EXT. SEINE—BATEAU MOUCHE—DUSK

The large motor launch, moving along the river, gaily ablaze with lights.

Med. shot—Reggie and Dyle (process) at a table for two by the rail, the city slowly passing in the b.g.

DYLE

(feels the cuff of his jacket)

Hey, you know this thing is still damp?

(pauses)

You haven't spoken a word for 20 minutes.

REGGIE

I was thinking about Charles and Scobie and who's going to be next, me? I don't suppose you know who the murderer is, do you?

DYLE

No, not yet.

REGGIE

Whoever's left alive at the end will pretty much have swen up the nomination, don't you think?

DYLE

What are you trying to say? That I might have killed Charles and Scobie? What I have to do to satisfy you? Become the next victim?

REGGIE

It's a start, anyway.

DYLE

(skeptical)

I can't understand you at all. One minute you're chasing me around the shower room and the next minute you're accusing me of murder.

REGGIE

Carson Dyle had no brother.

Wider angle. She rises from the table and walks to the rail. Dyle follows.

DYLE

Oh, I can explain that if you'll just listen.

REGGIE

I can't very well leave without a pair of water wings, can I?

DYLE

Alright, get set for the story of my life.

REGGIE

Fiction or nonfiction?

DYLE

Why don't you shut up?

REGGIE

Well!

DYLE

Are you going to listen?

REGGIE

Go on.

DYLE

All right. Now, when I was a young man, my father expected me to go into his business. Umbrella frames, that's what he made. Well, it's sensible business, I suppose. But I didn't have the sense in those days to be sensible.

REGGIE

I suppose all this is leading somewhere.

DYLE

Well, it led me away from my umbrella frames for one thing. But that left me without any honest means of support.

REGGIE

What do you mean?

DYLE

Well, in this highly competitive world, when a man has no profession, there isn't much choice. So I began looking for people who had more money than they needed, including some they barely miss.

REGGIE

(astonished)

You mean you're a thief?

DYLE

Well, that's not exactly the term I'd have chosen, but it sort of captures the spirit of the thing.

REGGIE

I don't believe it.

DYLE

I can't really blame you now.

REGGIE

But I do believe it—that's what I don't believe. So it's goodbye Alexander Dyle and welcome home Peter Joshua.

DYLE

Mm-Hmm. Sorry, the name's Adam Canfield.

REGGIE

Adam Canfield.

DYLE

(now called Adam)

Mm-Hmm.

REGGIE

Wonderful. Do you realize you've had three names in the past two days? I don't even know who I'm talking to anymore.

ADAM

Oh, man's the same. Even if the name isn't.

REGGIE

No, he isn't the same. Adam Canfield is a crook and I want to know why.

ADAM

Well, it's simple, I like what I do. I enjoy my work. There aren't many men in the world who would love their work as much as I do. You look around sometime.

REGGIE

Is there a Mrs. Canfield?

ADAM

Yes—

REGGIE & ADAM

—but we we're divorced.

ADAM

That's right. Now go and eat your dinner.

Another angle as they go back to the table.

REGGIE

Oh, I could eat a horse.

ADAM

(looking at all the food)

I think that's what you ordered.

REGGIE

Don't you dare be civil with me after leading me on like this.

ADAM

How did I lead you on?

REGGIE

(eating)

Oh, all that marvelous rejection. You knew I couldn't resist it. And now it turns out all you're interested in is the money.

BRIAN

That's right.

REGGIE

Oh!

ADAM

What would you like me to say? That a pretty girl with an outrageous manner means more to an all pro like me than a quarter of a million dollars?

REGGIE

I don't suppose so.

ADAM

It's a toss-up. I can tell you that.

REGGIE

(surprised)

What?

ADAM

Hasn't it occurred to you that I'm having a tough time keeping my hands off you?

(pauses)

Oh, you should see your face.

REGGIE

What's the matter with it?

ADAM

It's lovely.

Reggie sighs and drops her knife and fork.

ADAM

Now what's the trouble?

REGGIE

I'm not hungry anymore. Isn't it glorious?

The overhead lights go out.

REGGIE

Adam!

ADAM

It's all right. Come and look.

EXT. SEINE BATEAU MOUCHE—NIGHT

A searchlight near the boat's bridge has gone on and now begins sweeping the river banks. On benches by the water's edge, lovers are surprised by the bright light which suddenly and without warning discovers them in various attitudes of mutual affection. Some are embarrassed, some are amused and some (the most intimate) damn annoyed. One even shakes his fist at the light.

Med. shot—Reggie and Adam who, like everyone else, leave the table and stand together at the rail watching.

REGGIE

Hey, you don't look so bad in this light.

ADAM

Why do you think I brought you here?

REGGIE

(indicating the lovers)

I thought maybe you wanted me to see the kind of work the competition was turning out.

ADAM

Pretty good, huh? I taught them everything they do.

REGGIE

Oh, did they do that kind of thing *way* back in your day?

ADAM

Sure. How'd you think I got here?

She rises on tip-toes and kisses him gently; his only reaction is to look at her.

REGGIE

Not allowed to kiss back, huh?

ADAM

Oh, no. Doctor said it was bad for my thermostat.

She kisses him again. He responds a little better.

Well, when you come on, you come on, don't you?

REGGIE

Well, come on.

EXT. SEINE BATEAU MOUCHE—NIGHT

Wide shot—the brightly-lit boat floats away down the river.

INT. GIDEON'S ROOM—NIGHT

Med. shot—GIDEON, as he sits bolt upright in bed, startled. The room is dark and the phone is ringing. He switches on the lamp and picks up the receiver.

GIDEON

Yeah. Hmm? In the lobby?

(puts on his glasses and looks at his alarm clock)

Are you out of your mind or something? It's 3:30 in the morning. You mean it?

(sneezes)

All right. All right,I'll be right down. Wait a minute.

He hangs up, swings his feet out of bed and spears his slippers, reaching for his robe at the same time. Then he shuffles sleepily to the door.

INT. HOTEL CORRIDOR—THIRD FLOOR LANDING—NIGHT

As Gideon comes out of his room and goes to the elevator.

The cage is there. He opens the door and enters.

INT. ELEVATOR—NIGHT

Gideon closes the sliding grill and presses a button. The cage starts down. Gideon sneezes. Suddenly the elevator stops between floors and the lights go out.

GIDEON

Hey, hey, turn on the lights!

The lights go on again and the elevator passes out of sight, still going down, and passes the lobby

GIDEON

Hey, how do you stop this thing?

The elevator drops out of sight and we hear Gideon sneeze, multiple times, then scream.

The sleeping night porter, rudely awakened, walks to the elevator shaft. He opens the gate, pulls back the grill and the camera rushes past him to pick up Gideon below. His body is sitting on the floor of the cage, its grotesque sprawling attitude resembling a puppet's with its strings cut. Except that Gideon has no strings to cut—only a throat. From ear to ear.

INT. TEX'S ROOM—NIGHT

Medium shot—Grandpierre is in front of an empty bed, now doubly apoplectic. Camera zooms out to show Reggie and Adam in the doorway.

GRANDPIERRE

Three of them, all in their pajamas, they're ridiculous. What is it? Some new American fad? And now, your friend who lives here, the one from Texas. He's disappeared into the air. Where is he?

Close shot—Reggie and adam.

ADAM

I wish I knew.

GRANDPIERRE

Madame?

Reggie shrugs.

GRANDPIERRE

Tell me, Mr. Dyle, where were you at 3:30 AM?

ADAM

In my room, asleep.

GRANDPIERRE

And you, Mrs. Lampert.

REGGIE

I was too.

GRANDPIERRE

In Mr. Dyle's room?

REGGIE

No, in my room.

GRANDPIERRE

Obviously, you're telling the truth. For why would you invent such a ridiculous story? And if I were you, I wouldn't stay in my pajamas. Good night.

Grandpierre walks out between them. Reggie and Adam are still in the doorway.

ADAM

Well, that wraps it up. Tex has the money.

He urges her back toward her room and follows.

ADAM

You go to bed, I'll let you know when I found him.

REGGIE

You gonna go looking for him now?

ADAM

Well, if the police find him first, they're not going to turn over that quarter of a million dollars to us.

Reggie stops outside her room, Adam goes to his.

REGGIE

Oh, Adam.

ADAM

Do as I tell you. Go to bed and bolt your door.

They each enter their own room.

INT. ADAM'S ROOM—NIGHT

Adam enters, going to the closet to remove his suit. The phone rings. He answers it.

ADAM

Yeah.

INT. PHONE BOOTH—NIGHT

Close shot—Tex, as he speaks on the phone.

TEX

Now you listen to me, Dyle. Look, I know who's got that money, man, and I want my share. It seems to be growin' and growin' every day. Well, I ain't disappearing until I get it.

INT. ADAM'S ROOM—NIGHT

ADAM

(on the phone)

Where are you, Tex?

INT. PHONE BOOTH—NIGHT

TEX

(on the phone, laughs)

TEX

Come on, man. Look, my mama didn't raise no stupid children. I'll tell you what, you wanna find me, or you just look over your shoulder because from now on, I'm gonna be right behind you.

(hangs up)

INT. ADAM'S ROOM—NIGHT

Adam, hangs up the phone and knocks on Reggie's door.

ADAM

Open up.

INT. REGGIE'S ROOM—NIGHT

Reggie slips back into her robe and goes to the connecting door. She undoes the bolt and opens the door. Adam enters.

ADAM

I think I was wrong about Tex having the money.

REGGIE

Why?

ADAM

I just heard from him. He's still hungry. That means killing Gideon didn't get it for him. So he's narrowed it down to us. You've got it.

REGGIE

But I've looked everywhere. You know I have?

ADAM

(angry)

Where's the airlines bag.

REGGIE

In the wardrobe?

ADAM

Get it.

REGGIE

Lord, you're obstinate.

She goes to the closet and gets the bag.

ADAM

Charles must have had it with him on the train when Tex killed him. Thanks.

He takes the bag to the bed where he dumps out the contents.

REGGIE

Everybody and his Aunt Lilian have been through that bag, including me.

ADAM

Okay, we'll do it again.

REGGIE

I've been into it at least once a day. Somebody would've seen it.

Close shot—bed with Charles' belongings

ADAM'S VOICE (O.S.)

It's there, Reggie. We're looking at it right now. Something on that bed is worth a quarter of a million dollars.

REGGIE

But what?

ADAM

I don't know. I don't know.

Med. shot—Reggie and Adam as ADAM begins to examine the items one by one abd puts them back in the bag.

ADAM

Four passports. A steamship ticket. Anything in there?

REGGIE

Nothing.

ADAM

Wallet. Comb. Oh, a fountain pen. What about that key?

REGGIE

To the apartment, matches mine exactly.

Adam picks up a letter and takes his glasses from his robe to read it. Reggie takes his glasses from him.

REGGIE

Oh, I bet you don't really need those.

She puts them on and takes them off quickly, surprised.

REGGIE

You need them.

She hands them back to him.

ADAM

(reading)

Well, it still doesn't make sense, but it isn't worth a quarter of a million dollars either.

REGGIE

(holding the tooth powder cannister)

Wait a minute.

ADAM

What?

REGGIE

The tooth powder.

ADAM

What about it?

REGGIE

Could you recognize heroin just by the taste of it?

He shakes some powder into his hand and tastes it. Reggie watches expectantly.

ADAM

Heroin, peppermint-flavored heroin.

REGGIE

(frowns)

Hmm. Well, I guess that's it. Dead end.

Adam re-zips the bag and brings it back to the closet.

ADAM

Well, go to bed. You've gotta get up and go to work in the morning. There's nothing more we can do tonight.

REGGIE

I love you, Adam.

ADAM

Yes, you told me.

REGGIE

No, the last time I said I love you, Alex.

ADAM

Oh.

(pauses)

Oh.

He returns to his room.

EXT. EURESCO BUILDING—ESTABLISHING—DAY

A modern glass and concrete structure.

INT. EURESCO CONFERENCE ROOM—DAY

Several delegates identified by little plaques in front of them listing their respective nations, and their aides, sit around the large table. They are all wearing earphones.

The Italian delegate is speaking.

DELEGATE

—e questo è molto importante per il Governo che io ho l'onore di rappresentare disturberebbe l'esportazione delle derrate farinose italiane in questa parte del mondo. Signori Delegati vi ringrazio della vostra attenzione.

INT. REGGIE'S BOOTH—DAY

Reggie, wearing her headset, is talking with Sylvie.

REGGIE

Hold it. They're recognizing Great Britain.

INT. EURESCO CONFERENCE ROOM—DAY

BRITAIN DELEGATE (O.S.)

Mr. Chairman, fellow delegates, my distinguished colleague from Italy. Her Majesty's delegation has listened with great patience to the Southern European—

Past the delegates we see the translators' booths with Reggie to the right. Sylvie, in a hurry, enters her booth in the middle. Adam enters Reggie's booth and sits down next to her.

INT. REGGIE'S BOOTH—DAY

ADAM

(sees she's wearing a headset)

Oh, are you on?

REGGIE

(removes part of her headset)

No, it's all right. What's wrong, Adam?

ADAM

Nothing's wrong. I think I found something. I was snooping around Tex's room and came across this in the wastebasket. I stuck it together again.

He shows her the taped-together paper.

REGGIE

That's the receipt Grandpierre gave me for Charles' things. I don't see how that's going to—

ADAM

No, you're not looking. Last night when we went through the airlines bag, something was missing, an agenda. That's an appointment book, isn't it? It wasn't there.

Insert as he again shows her the police receipt, the one Grandpierre gave Reggie. He points to the first listed item, *UN AGENDA*

REGGIE

That's right. I remember Grandpierre looking through it, but there was nothing in it. At least nothing the police thought was very important.

ADAM

Can you remember anything in it at all?

REGGIE

Well, he did say something about Charles' last appointment.

ADAM

With whom? Where?

REGGIE

I think it only said where.

ADAM

Now come on, Reggie—think. Think! This may be what we're looking for.

REGGIE

Adam, that money doesn't belong to us. If we keep, it'll be breaking the law!

ADAM

Well, nonsense. We didn't steal it, there's no law against stealing stolen money.

REGGIE

Of course there is.

ADAM

There is?

REGGIE

Yes.

ADAM

When did they pass such a silly law? Now think Reggie—what was in that appointment book?

REGGIE

Oh, it was a place or a street corner or something. Watch it, I am on.

FRENCH DELEGATE

Mess. les delegues, mes collegues distingues de la Grande Bretagne, Mr. Delegate, le probleme qui se presente . . .

She turns back to the conference, flips a switch and starts speaking into her headset. As she translates, Adam leans in and nuzzles her neck.

REGGIE

Of the Western Hemisphere Conference . . .

(distracted)

Of the Western Hemisphere Conference held on March 22nd . . .

(stops and turns toward Adam)

No wait—it was last Thursday, 5 o'clock, the Jardin des Champs-Elysees. That's it, Adam, the garden!

Through the window we see the delegates turn around, confused, some rising from their chairs.

ADAM

Well, it's Thursday today and it's almost 5 o'clock. So come on.

He stands up to leave and pulls Reggie along with him.

ADAM

(pausing to address the delegates through her headset)

Oh, it's alright, gentlemen. Carry on.

EXT. GUIGNOL—LATE AFTERNOON

Two shot—Reggie and Adam by the locked gate.

REGGIE

Now what?

ADAM

Five o'clock Thursday, the gardens. It must be something around here.

REGGIE

Charles' appointment was last week.

ADAM

Yes I know, but this is all we got left.

REGGIE

You're not kidding, ten minutes ago I had a job.

They walkaway from the gate.

ADAM

But now you've got another job. So stop grumbling and start looking. I'll take that side. You poke around over here.

They split up.

Various shots, Adam's p.o.v.—a quick succession showing: 1. Children's merry-go-round, 2. Busy playground with children's swings, 3. A gendarme giving directions, 4. A man crossing the street in front of a line of horse carriages, 4. Children being loaded into small donkey carts.

Adam pauses at the center of the park, thinking. Reggie joins him.

REGGIE

It is hopeless. I don't even know what we are looking for.

ADAM

I don't think Tex does either.

REGGIE

Tex, is he here?

ADAM

Look.

Med. shot—Tex, who stands at the other side of the merry-go-round, looking at something in his hand: Charles' agenda. Now he closes it and walks away, disappearing behind a hedge.

ADAM

I'm going to see what he's up to. You stay here.

Adam starts off.

REGGIE

Be careful, Adam, he's already killed three men.

EXT. RUE GABRIEL—LATE AFTERNOON

Between the curb and the Jardin, two rows of wooden booths have been set up. They have collected quite a crowd. Into this area comes Tex, followed at a safe distance by Adam. Suddenly Tex stops.

Close shot—Tex as he stares wide-eyed at something.

Close shot—stamps neatly displayed on a counter of one of the booths.

Close shot—Tex, as he wheels to look at another booth.

Close shot—more stamps in another arrangement.

Close shot—Tex turns crazily to look at another booth, then another.

Close shot—even more stamps, various flash shots of stamps of all sizes, shapes and colors.

Med. shot—Tex as he understands. He turns to rush off and bumps smack into Adam, not realizing it's him.

He rushes off past Adam, who watches him for a moment, confused, then turns toward the booth, not yet having seen the stamps.

Med. shot—booth from Adam's angle. There are one or two persons standing at the booth. Camera zooms in on multiple displays of stamps.

Close shot—Adam as he quickly turns to find Tex.

Med. shot—Tex as he pushes another man away and hops into the back of the taxi he's hailed. It pulls away from the curb as Adam runs towards it.

ADAM

(at Tex's taxi)

Wait! Wait!!

Adam pushes the same man aside, again taking his taxi, and jumps inside.

Med. shot—Reggie wandering in front of the merry-go-round, unaware.

INT. HOTEL CORRIDOR—THIRD FLOOR LANDING—LATE AFTERNOON

As Adam comes up the stairs and goes to Reggie's door. Whipping out his gun, he flings it open.

INT. REGGIE'S ROOM—LATE AFTERNOON

Adam enters and finds Tex sits in a chair next to the bed, rolling a cigarette. On the bed is the airlines bag, its contents dumped on the floor.

ADAM

Alright, where's the letter?

TEX

The letter, huh? It ain't worth nothing.

ADAM

You know what I mean. The envelope with the stamps on it. I want it.

TEX

You greenhorn . . . Why you thick skull, hair-brain, half-witted, greenhorn. And they was both too smart for us!

ADAM

What are you talking about?

TEX

Oh, first her husband, now her? She batted all of them big eyes at you and you fell for it like an egg from a tall chicken. You want the envelope?

Adam takes it and looks at it.

Insert—envelope, the corner containing the stamps is missing, torn off.

Med. shot—Adam and Tex

TEX

There, you take it. It's all yours. You kill all three of them for nothing.

(laughs hysterically)

You greenhorn, you blockheaded jackass! You a nincompoop!

EXT. ROND POINT—LATE AFTERNOON

Sylvie is sitting alone on a bench near the stamp market, reading a newspaper. Reggie approaches her.

REGGIE

Sylvie, what are you doing here?

SYLVIE

(stands)

I'm waiting for Jean-Louis.

REGGIE

Oh, what's he up to?

SYLVIE

Oh, he was so excited when he got the stamps you gave him this morning. He said he'd never seen any like them.

REGGIE

I'm glad. What's all this?

(nods toward the wooden booths)

SYLVIE

The stamp market, it's there every Thursday afternoon. That's where Jean-Louis trades his stamps.

REGGIE

(grabs Sylvie by the arms)

Good lord—where is he?

SYLVIE

What's the matter, Cherie?

They rush off into the market.

REGGIE

The stamps, they're worth a fortune!

SYLVIE

What?

REGGIE

A fortune. Come on. . . .

Traveling two shot—Reggie and Sylvie as they run past the booths, looking around.

REGGIE

(stopping)

I don't see him anywhere.

SYLVIE

We'll separate. You look over there.

REGGIE

Okay.

They go off in opposite directions.

Med. shot—Reggie as she hurries along a row of stalls, weaving around small groups of men standing together, showing each other stamps.

Med. shot—Sylvie searching in another section of the market.

SYLVIE

Jean-Louis!

REGGIE

Jean-Louis—!

Med. shot—Reggie spots a boy, runs to him and spins him around. It's not Jean-Louis.

Med. shot—Sylvie.

SYLVIE

Jean-Louis!

She spots Jean-Louis at a stand, looking at some stamps. Sylvie grabs him.

Med. shot—REGGIE, still searching.

SYLVIE (O.S.)

(calling)

Reggie! Reggie!

Reggie runs up and joins them.

REGGIE

Jean-Louis, thank heaven. Do you have the . . .

She takes a large sack of assorted stamps from his hand and looks at it.

REGGIE

What's this?

JEAN-LOUIS

A man gave me all those for only three.

REGGIE

A man? Oh no, Jean-Louis! Who? Where?

SYLVIE

Vite, mon cheri, vite. Quickly, my darling, quickly.

JEAN-LOUIS

(points down the row of booths)

La-bas!

REGGIE

Come on.

They all run off towards where he was pointing.

Med. shot—stamp booth that's closed, a tarp drawn down over it. A sign above it says *Mson FELIX*

SYLVIE

Oh, but he's gone.

REGGIE

I don't blame him.

INT. FÉLIX'S ROOM—DUSK

Close shot—Félix, a man in his sixties, holds a magnifying glass in his hand, busy studying something on the desk in front of him. There is a knock. He looks up. Another knock.

FÉLIX

Entrez.

The door opens and Reggie, followed by Sylvie and Jean-Louis, enters. The office is cozy and well-appointed with stamp displays covering the walls.

REGGIE

Mr. Felix.

FÉLIX

Oui, I was expecting you. I knew you would come.

Close shot—Reggie, downcast

FÉLIX (O.S.)

Look at them, madam. Have you ever in your entire life seen anything so beautiful?

REGGIE

I'm sorry, I don't know anything about stamps.

Med. shot—Reggie, Félix, Sylvie and Jean-Louis

FÉLIX

I know them as one knows his own face, though I had never seen them.

Insert—stamps, three of them—still attached to the portion of the torn envelope. He indicates the first one with tongs.

FÉLIX (O.S.)

This one, a Swedish four shilling called Den Gula Fyraskill-ingen, printed in 1854.

Med. shot—Reggie standing in front of his desk.

REGGIE

What is it worth?

FÉLIX

Well, the money is unimportant.

REGGIE

I'm afraid it's very important.

FÉLIX

In your money, perhaps $85,000.

REGGIE

May I sit down?

FÉLIX

Please.

(she sits)

REGGIE

And the blue one.

Insert—the middle stamp.

FÉLIX (O.S.)

Oh, it's called the Hawaiian Blue. In 1894, the owner was murdered by a rival collector who was obsessed to own it.

Med. shot—Reggie, leaning in.

REGGIE

And what is its value today?

FÉLIX

65,000.

REGGIE

And the last one?

FÉLIX

The best for a last. *Le chef-d'oeuvre de la collection.* The masterpiece. It's the most valuable stamp in the world.

Insert—the last stamp.

It's called the Gazette Moldave. It was printed by hand on colored paper and marked with the initials of the printer. Today it has a value of a hundred thousand dollars.

Med. shot—over Reggie's shoulder, Félix at his desk.

FÉLIX

I'm not a thief, madam. I knew there was some mistake.

REGGIE

You gave the boy a great many stamps in return. Are they for sale now?

FÉLIX

Oh, let me see. 350 European, 200 Asian, 175 American, a hundred African, and 12 Princess Grace commemorative. Which comes to 10 francs. And don't forget these.

Félix uses his tongs to hand her the envelope fragment.

REGGIE

Thank you. I'm sorry.

Close shot—Félix.

FÉLIX

Oh no, for a few minutes they were mine. That is enough.

INT. HOTEL CORRIDOR—THIRD FLOOR LANDING—NIGHT

As Reggie comes hurrying up the stairs. She goes first to Adam's room and knocks.

REGGIE

Adam? Adam?

There is no answer. She goes to her own door and, to her surprise, finds it ajar.

INT. REGGIE'S ROOM—NIGHT

Reggie enters then freezes, having seen something on the floor.

Med. shot—Tex's body lies on the floor, the wrists of his extended arms tied to the leg of the bed, his ankles to the steam radiator. And tied around his head is a plastic, transparent bag, inside of which the suffocated man's face, the eyes bulging against the plastic

clinging tight to his features, can be seen all too clearly. Reggie enters the shot, bending down to see if he's alive. Then she sees something beside his hands near the leg of the bed.

Close shot—carpet. With his dying effort, Tex has traced a name against the grain of the maroon carpet—*DYLE*.

Close shot—Reggie, astonished and horrified.

Wider angle as she gets to her feet and hurries to the phone.

INT. BARTHOLOMEW'S APARTMENT—NIGHT

Bartholomew, his face lathered for a shaving, steps into the bedroom to answer the phone.

BARTHOLOMEW

(on the phone)

Hello?

INT. REGGIE'S ROOM—NIGHT

REGGIE

(on the phone)

Mr. Bartholomew?

BARTHOLOMEW (V.O.)

Yes?

REGGIE

Tex is dead, smothered.

(pauses, shaking)

And Adam did it. He killed them all.

INT. BARTHOLOMEW'S APARTMENT—NIGHT

BARTHOLOMEW

Are you sure?

INT. REGGIE'S ROOM—NIGHT

REGGIE

Yes, I'm sure. Tex wrote the word Dyle before he died. He's the murderer. I tell you.

INT. BARTHOLOMEW'S APARTMENT—NIGHT

BARTHOLOMEW

Now, wait a minute. Just a minute, Mrs. Lampert, you better give that to me again.

INT. REGGIE'S ROOM—NIGHT

REGGIE

It was the stamps on the letter Charles had with him on the train. They were there in plain view all the time, but no one bothered to look at the envelope.

BARTHOLOMEW (V.O.)

Now, Mrs. Lampert, listen to me, you're not safe as long as you have these stamps.

INT. BARTHOLOMEW'S APARTMENT—NIGHT

Let's see . . . Do you know the Cinegarden at the Palais Royale?

REGGIE (V.O.)

Yes, the Colonnade?

BARTHOLOMEW

Yes, by the Colonnade. As fast as you can get there. Hurry, Mrs. Lampert!

INT. REGGIE'S ROOM—NIGHT

REGGIE

I'm leaving right away. Goodbye.

INT. HOTEL CORRIDOR—THIRD LANDING—NIGHT

As Reggie leaves her room and goes to the elevator. She presses the button, then notices it is in use. She goes to the stairs and starts down.

INT. HOTEL STAIRCASE—NIGHT

Between the landings. The stairs curve around the open elevator shaft. As Reggie comes down the stairs, the cage rises into view. Inside is Adam. For a moment, she stops and their eyes meet.

ADAM

Reggie! The stamps, where are they?! Reggie! Wait!

INT. HOTEL STAIRWAY—NIGHT

Between the first landing and the lobby. Reggie running down the stairs, the elevator following.

REGGIE

Why? So you can kill me too? Tex is dead, he wrote Dyle on the carpet!

ADAM

I'm not Dyle, and you know that!

REGGIE

Tex doesn't know that. You're a murderer!

ADAM

Reggie, I want those stamps!

INT. HOTEL LOBBY—NIGHT

Reggie reaches the lobby first and, without hesitation, races toward the front door and out. The elevator, Adam inside, has not yet reached the bottom.

EXT. HOTEL LOBBY—NIGHT

A taxi stands by the curb. Reggie leaves the hotel and runs to it.

REGGIE

(indicating the direction)

Le Palais Royale, vite.

CAB DRIVER

Je suis occupe.

REGGIE

Mais c'est tres urgent!

CAB DRIVER

Occupe.

She looks around and sees Adam come out of the hotel and straight toward her. She turns and runs off toward the Place St. Michel.

EXT. PLACE ST. MICHEL—NIGHT

As Reggie comes to the corner she stops, sees the Métro station entrance ("St. Michel") and rushes down the stairs. Adam is behind her.

INT. ST. MICHEL MÉTRO STATION—NIGHT

Reggie runs down the stairs, goes to the booth and buys a ticket, casting a quick look behind her. Adam just coming off the stairs, runs after her.

He goes to buy a ticket as well but is delayed by the man ahead of him.

INT. MÉTRO TICKET GATE—NIGHT

Reggie gets to the gate ahead of Adam. Barely stopping, she holds out her ticket to the guard to be punched, then heads down the platform, still running. Adam gets to the gate but the guard grabs his sleeve as he tries to run through.

GUARD

Whoa, Monsieur!

Adam steps back to have his ticket punched, losing sight of Reggie.

INT. MÉTRO PASSAGEWAY—NIGHT

Camera leading Reggie as she runs, the passageway nearly empty. Her footsteps echo against the tile and concrete walls. She goes down the stairs onto the platform, anxiously looking down the tunnel for the train. Camera pans sharply, 180 degrees, to pick up Adam rounding the corner in hot pursuit.

INT. MÉTRO PLATFORM—NIGHT

Reggie starts down the platform, looking behind her every few steps. Suddenly she looks up in surprise—there, across the tracks on the opposite platform is Adam. He has evidently made the wrong turn back in the passageway.

They stare at each other for a moment. Then the bell rings, announcing the arrival of a train. Adam turns, running back through the exit behind him. Not knowing what to do, Reggie looks into the darkness of the tunnel. The approaching train can be heard.

REGGIE

(to herself)

Come on—please—

She turns to look at the gate—slowly, the pneumatic door starts to close. As it does, the train roars into the station.

INT. MÉTRO PASSAGEWAY—NIGHT

The gate can be seen slowly closing. Adam runs to it, tries to force it back and barely squeezes through.

INT. MÉTRO PLATFORM—NIGHT

Reggie enters the center car, as Adam, just behind her, manages to make it onto the last car. The doors shut in unison, the latches falling with a concerted click and the little whistle blowing to inform the motor-man to depart. The train starts to move.

INT. MÉTRO CAR—NIGHT

Reggie hides behind the last seat, fearful. Thinking Adam was left on the platform, she relaxes and takes a seat.

INT. MÉTRO CAR—NIGHT

Adam starts to weave his way past the other passengers, on his way to the center car. He tries to open the door between them but it's locked. Adam looks up and they see each other.

Reggie gets up and goes to the doors.

INT. MÉTRO CAR—NIGHT

Adam sees what she's doing and does the same.

INT. MÉTRO PLATFORM—NIGHT

Adam hurries off the train, looking for Reggie. He finds his way blocked by five nuns in large, white butterfly hats. It takes him a few precious seconds to work his way around them. He runs upstairs.

INT. MÉTRO SORTIE—NIGHT

Adam enters a deserted area, no sign of Reggie. He pauses then runs off down a corridor to the right. Camera pans to a phone booth (solid door with a window in the upper half) and we see Reggie's hand reaching up to dial a number.

INT. PHONE BOOTH—NIGHT

Reggie sits on the floor of the booth, dialing.

INT. EMBASSY SWITCHBOARD—NIGHT

An operator speaking into a headset.

OPERATOR

American Embassy.

INT. PHONE BOOTH—NIGHT

REGGIE

(whispering)

American Embassy, Mr. Bartholomew's office, please.

INT. EMBASSY SWITCHBOARD—NIGHT

OPERATOR

Would you speak a little louder, please?

INT. PHONE BOOTH—NIGHT

REGGIE

I can't speak any louder. Mr. Hamilton Bartholomew.

INT. EMBASSY SWITCHBOARD—NIGHT

OPERATOR

I'm sorry. Mr. Bartholomew has left for the day.

INT. PHONE BOOTH—NIGHT

REGGIE

But someone's trying to kill me!

EMBASSY OPERATOR (V.O.)

What?

REGGIE

Kill me! You've gotta get word to him right away. He's in the center garden of the Palais Royale near the Colonnade. Tell him I'm trapped in a phone booth right below him in the metro station, and the name is Lampert.

Reggie hangs up the phone.

INT. MÉTRO STATION—NIGHT

Adam is still running around the station, searching for Reggie. He reaches a locked gate —a dead end—and doubles back.

INT. MÉTRO SORTIE—NIGHT

Adam comes around the corner and slows down as he heads towards Reggie's booth.

INT. PHONE BOOTH—NIGHT

Reggie is crouching, listening, and her eyes go wide as she sees Adam pass by. She stands up slowly and watches as he heads for the stairs to the platform.

INT. MÉTRO SORTIE—NIGHT

Reggie flees the booth and heads for a gate but it's locked. She turns and runs in the other direction.

INT—PRIVATE CLUB

Close shot of a phone ringing and a hand lifting it up. Camera pulls back and tracks upward to reveal an unfamiliar man in a suit—the *real* Mr. Bartholomew.

MR. BARTHOLOMEW

(*on the phone*)

Hello?

EMBASSY OPERATOR (V.O.)

Hello, Mr. Bartholomew?

MR. BARTHOLOMEW

Yes?

INT. EMBASSY SWITCHBOARD—NIGHT

EMBASSY OPERATOR

There was a call for you just now, Mr. Bartholomew. It sounded quite urgent. A Mrs. Lampert

INT—PRIVATE CLUB

MR. BARTHOLOMEW

Lampert, I don't know any Mrs. Lampert.

EMBASSY OPERATOR

She says she's trapped in a metro station and someone's trying to kill her.

MR. BARTHOLOMEW

Trying to kill her? Who does she think I am? The CIA? Alright, I guess you better call the French police.

EXT. PALAIS ROYAL COURTYARD—COLONNADE—NIGHT

The smaller court at the Comédie-Française end of the Palais gardens, separated from the larger garden by a double peristyle consisting of two twin rows (these separated from each other by a small marble court) of twenty columns each—in all, eighty columns.

The only person in sight is the man we have known as Bartholomew, walking slowly through the columns, looking into the distance expectantly.

INT. MÉTRO PLATFORM—NIGHT

Adam is at the bottom of the stairs, searching the platform. He looks towards the far end then turns around and starts walking in the other direction.

Another angle, overhead shot of Adam slowly stalking the platform

INT. MÉTRO SORTIE—NIGHT

Reggie, leaves the phone booth and runs to the stairway down to the platform.

INT. MÉTRO PLATFORM—NIGHT

Adam turns to look at the oncoming train and sees REGGIE coming off the stairs.

Close shot of Reggie, alarmed.

Med. shot as the train pulls into the station and the doors open, Reggie running past with Adam in pursuit.

Camera pans to the far stairs as Reggie runs up them, Adam right behind her.

EXT. PLACE PALAIS ROYAL—NIGHT

Reggie comes up the stairs from the Métro then runs across the street, ignoring the traffic, toward the Rue de Valois (which forms one side of the Palais Royal). Adam is still right behind her.

EXT. PALAIS ROYAL COURTYARD—COLONNADE—NIGHT

From the Rue de Valois side of the Palais, Reggie runs into the court, she glances back and sees Adam following.

Reverse shot as spots "Bartholomew" at the far corner and runs towards him.

REGGIE

Mr. Bartholomew! Mr. Bartholomew!! Help me.

ADAM

(stops and pulls his gun)

Reggie! Stop! That man is Carson Dyle.

Wide shot as both "Bartholomew" and Adam step behind the stone columns at opposite ends of the colonnade, keeping out of each other's sight. Reggie stands out in the open, confused as to which man she should go to.

Close shots on each as they speak:

"BARTHOLOMEW"

We all know Carson Dyle is dead, Mrs. Lampert.

ADAM

I tell you, he's Carson Dyle!

"BARTHOLOMEW"

Well, you're not gonna believe him. Just bring those stamps over here. He's trying to trick you again.

ADAM

Tex recognized him—that's why he wrote Dyle. If you take him those stamps, he'll kill you too.

Reggie looks towards Adam.

"BARTHOLOMEW"

Mrs. Lampert, if I'm who he says I am, what's preventing me from killing you right now?

ADAM

Because he'd have to come out to get the stamps. And he knows he'll never make it.

"BARTHOLOMEW"

Mrs. Lampert, he wants the money for himself. That's all he is ever wanted.

Wide shot from behind Adam's shoulder of Reggie in the distance.

REGGIE

He's with the CIA. I saw him at the embassy.

ADAM

I tell you, he's Carson Dyle!

Reverse shot from behind "bartholomew", Reggie in the distance.

"BARTHOLOMEW"

(sarcastic)

That's right, Mrs. Lampert. That's right, I'm a dead man—look at me.

Close shots on each as they speak:

REGGIE

(looks back and forth, anguished)

Oh! I don't know who anybody is!

ADAM

Reggie, I beg you—just trust me once more.

REGGIE

Why should I?

ADAM

I can't think of a reason in the world why you should.

"BARTHOLOMEW"

Stop right now, Mrs. Lampert, or I'll kill you!

ADAM

It won't get you the stamps, Dyle! You'll still have to come out to get them! And I'm not likely to miss at this range!

"BARTHOLOMEW"

(now called **CARSON***)*

Maybe not, but it takes a lot of bullets to kill me—they left me there with five of them in my legs and my stomach. Mrs. Lampert, they knew I was still alive, but they left me there! I spent 10 months in a German prison camp with nothing to stop the pain. They left me there, Mrs. Lampert, they deserved to die!

Wide shot from behind carson, Reggie in the distance.

REGGIE

I had nothing to do with it!

Tracking shot from behind Adam as he creeps over to the second set of columns, putting himself behind "Bartholomew" while he talks.

CARSON (O.S.)

You've got the money now. It belongs to me. Mrs. Lampert, they knew I was still alive, but they left me there. That's why I had to kill them, all four of them. Please believe me, Mrs. Lampert, I'll kill you too.

Close shot of Reggie, frozen with fear.

Close shot of Carson

CARSON

It won't make any difference. It's no use. You're running out of time. I've come too far to turn back, I swear I'll kill you! Make up your mind, Mrs. Lampert—now.

Close shot of Reggie.

REGGIE

(screams)

Adam!

Med. shot—Adam as he aims and fires.

Carson takes off running through the columns as Adam fires again. Adam follows him and we see Carson is running after Reggie.

EXT. COMÉDIE FRANÇAISE—STAGE DOOR—NIGHT

Reggie stops and opens a door and ducks inside. Carson is right behind her, enters and slams the door behind him, locking it.

INT. COMÉDIE FRANÇAISE—NIGHT

Carson steps carefully into the theater.

Wider shot of the magnificent auditorium, Carson alone.

EXT. COMÉDIE FRANÇAISE—STAGE DOOR—NIGHT

Adam arrives, tries the door but it's locked. He takes off running back in the direction he came.

INT. COMÉDIE FRANÇAISE—ORCHESTRA—NIGHT

Carson walks slowly down the aisle towards the stage, gun drawn, looking between the seats.

EXT. PALAIS ROYAL COURTYARD—COLONNADE—NIGHT

Adam running through the columns.

INT. COMÉDIE FRANÇAISE—STAGE—NIGHT

Carson climbs up onto the stage and heads into the wing, where he turns on the stage lights.

EXT. PALAIS ROYAL COURTYARD—COLONNADE—NIGHT

Adam finds another entrance and opens the door.

INT. COMÉDIE FRANÇAISE—TRAPROOM—NIGHT

Adam enters at the top of a double staircase, backstage. It's a massive room, lit dimly from above, with myriad stairways and scaffolding that casts shadows on every surface.

INT. COMÉDIE FRANÇAISE—STAGE—NIGHT

As Carson moves carefully across the darkened stage near the footlights, looking for Reggie. At mid-stage, the camera pans down to his feet, only a few inches from the prompter's box.

Inside, huddling down, is a terrified Reggie, holding her breath as she watches him. He walks past her and she exhales with relief.

Close shot of her trying the door but it's locked.

INT. TRAPROOM—NIGHT

Adam descends the stairs, slow and quiet.

INT. STAGE—NIGHT

Carson checks behind the curtain at stage right and heads backstage.

INT. TRAPROOM—NIGHT

Adam has reached the floor and looks around, slowly. He stops and looks up as he hears Carson from above.

INT. BACKSTAGE—NIGHT

Carson walks past a scenic backdrop.

INT. TRAPROOM—NIGHT

Adam is looking up, having heard the footsteps on the stage over his head—and hearing them now. He looks around and sees a narrow, curving staircase leading up. He goes to it, and, starting up, finds a door. He tries the knob—the door is locked.

Close shot as the handle goes up and down uselessly—it's the same one Reggie was struggling with from inside the prompt box.

INT. STAGE—NIGHT

Carson, upstage, looking behind a piece of classic scenery, hears the doorknob and turns suddenly. From Carson's p.o.v. we catch a quick glimpse of Reggie as she ducks down out of sight. Too late.

Close shot—Carson looking down at her.

CARSON

Alright, I know you're in there, Mrs. Lampert, come on out.

INT. TRAPROOM—NIGHT

Adam hears Carson and stops trying to open the door, listening.

CARSON (O.S.)

Do you hear me? Come on out!

Adam comes down the stairs from the prompter's box and looks up at the ceiling.

Med. shot—the ceiling is divided into thirty-six square sections, each numbered and lettered—from 1A to 6F. They are trapdoors.

Med. Shot—Adam looks from the ceiling to a row of levers on one wall.

Close shot—levers, thirty-six of them, numbered and lettered to correspond to the traps.

INT. STAGE—NIGHT

As Carson takes a few steps towards the prompter's box, his gun ready.

CARSON

I don't wanna kill you, but I will. Come on out. The game is over, Mrs. Lampert.

INT. TRAPROOM—NIGHT

Adam is listening carefully, trying to figure out where CARSON is standing, watching the ceiling.

Close shot—trap is marked C-4.

CARSON (O.S.)

I won't wait much longer, Mrs. Lampert.

Med. shot—Adam as he turns to the levers and reaches for the one marked C- 4. He is about to pull it.

INT. STAGE—NIGHT

Med. shot—Carson takes a few more steps forward.

INT. PROMPTER'S BOX—NIGHT

Close shot—Reggie huddled inside.

INT. TRAPROOM—NIGHT

Adam stops himself from pulling the lever just in time. He lets his held breath escape. He looks back at the ceiling.

Close shot—trap marked C-4. Camera moves to the next trap, marked D-4.

CARSON (O.S.)

I know you're in there, Mrs. Lampert—

Med. shot—Adam looks at the lever marked D-4. He is perspiring heavily. He slowly reaches for the lever.

INT. STAGE—NIGHT

Close shot—Carson's feet as he stops on a trapdoor.

Close shot—Carson aiming his gun down toward Reggie in the prompter's box.

CARSON

Game over, Mrs. Lampert.

INT. TRAPROOM—NIGHT

Adam pulls the lever.

INT. STAGE—NIGHT

Carson drops through the trapdoor, screaming.

INT. TRAPROOM—NIGHT

Carson lands on hard on the floor and lands face down, not moving.

Carson is about to move closer to the prompter's box when suddenly the stage under him opens and he plummets through out of sight. At the same time we hear a shot.

INT. STAGE—NIGHT

Close shot—prompter's box as Reggie slowly peers out.

Med. shot—open trap from above, over Reggie's head. She can see Carson sprawled on the floor below, face down and dead. Adam goes over to the body and looks up at Reggie.

EXT. RUE DE RIVOLI—NIGHT

As a taxi rolls by the arcades, camera panning with it.

INT. TAXI—NIGHT (PROCESS)

Reggie and Adam in the rear of the cab. Reggie has one of her feet in her hand, shoe off, rubbing it.

REGGIE

You didn't have to chase me so hard.

(looks at her foot in his hands)

That one's done, do this one.

ADAM

Oh.

REGGIE

I'm sorry, I thought you were the murderer. How was I to know he was as big a liar as you are?

ADAM

Is that all the gratitude I get for saving your hide? Here, rub your own blinking foot.

(lets go of her foot)

REGGIE

The truth now—was it my hide or those stamps?

ADAM

Well, what a terrible thing to say. How could you think that?

REGGIE

Then prove it to me. Tell me to go to the embassy first thing in the morning and turn in those stamps.

Adam says nothing.

REGGIE

I said, tell me to go to the embassy first thing—

ADAM

Alright, I heard you. I heard you. I heard you.

REGGIE

Then say it.

ADAM

Now Reggie, listen to me—there's something I'd like to explain.

REGGIE

Never mind, I'll go by myself.

ADAM

Well, what makes you think they're even interested? It's only a quarter of a million dollars. It'll cost more than that for them to fix up their bookkeeping. Now, as a taxpayer—

EXT. AMERICAN EMBASSY—MAIN ENTRANCE—DAY

Reggie and Adam approach a Marine in full-dress uniform, always on guard at the Embassy.

REGGIE

(to Adam)

Who's a taxpayer? Crooks don't pay taxes.

(to the Marine)

Excuse me, soldier.

MARINE

Marine, ma'am.

REGGIE

Oh, forgive me. Who would I see regarding the return of stolen government money?

MARINE

Well, you might try the Treasury Department, ma'am. Room 217, second floor, Mr. Cruikshank.

REGGIE

217, thank you, Marine.

INT. EMBASSY CORRIDOR—DAY

Reggie and Adam step out of an elevator and walk past a door marked *PRIVATE* to a door marked 217.

ADAM

Uh, uh . . . Do you mind if I don't go in with you? The sight of all that money being given away might make me break out.

Reggie looks back at him and then opens the door.

INT. EMBASSY TREASURY OFFICE—DAY

A secretary sits behind a desk. She looks up as Reggie enters, alone.

REGGIE

Mr. Cruikshank, please, my name is Lampert.

MRS. FOSTER

Yes. Mr. Cruikshank, a Ms. Lamp—

REGGIE

Mrs.

MRS. FOSTER

Mrs. Lampert to see you? Yes sir. Go right in.

REGGIE

Thank you.

Reggie goes to the door leading to the private office.

INT. CRUIKSHANK'S OFFICE—DAY

Featuring the door as Reggie enters. She stops suddenly.

Another angle featuring the desk. Behind it sits Adam (now Cruikshank), who smiles and makes a funny face.

Reggie closes the door behind her.

REGGIE

Of all the mean, rotten, contemptible crooked—

CRUIKSHANK

Crooked? I think you'd be glad to find out I'm not crooked.

REGGIE

You can't even be honest about being dishonest. Why didn't you say something?

CRUIKSHANK

We're not allowed to tell. Come on, give me the stamps.

REGGIE

Wait a minute—how did Carson Dyle get an office in this building anyway?

CRUIKSHANK

Well, when did you meet him? What time of the day, I mean?

REGGIE

About one.

CRUIKSHANK

The lunch hour. Probably worked it out in advance. Found an office usually left open and just moved in for the time you were here.

REGGIE

Then how do I know this is your office?

CRUIKSHANK

(picking up the phone)

Mrs. Foster, take a memo to Bartholomew in security recommending—

REGGIE

Bartholomew.

CRUIKSHANK

—recommending that embassy offices be kept locked during the lunch hour.

REGGIE

(sits down)

Starting with his own.

Cruikshank gets up and comes around the side of the desk.

CRUIKSHANK

Now, give me the stamps, come on.

REGGIE

And what's your first name today?

CRUIKSHANK

Brian.

REGGIE

Brian Cruikshank. Serves me right if I get stuck with that one.

Cruikshank sits down on the edge of the desk.

CRUIKSHANK

Well, who asked you to get stuck with any of them? Come on.

REGGIE

Is there a Mrs. Cruikshank?

CRUIKSHANK

Yes.

REGGIE

But we are divorced.

CRUIKSHANK

No.

Takes out his wallet and removes a picture, shows it to Reggie.

CRUIKSHANK

My mother, she lives in Detroit. You'd like her. She'd like you too. Come on, give me those stamps.

REGGIE

Not until you prove to me that you're really Brian Cruikshank.

CRUIKSHANK

One day next week, I'll put it on a marriage license. How about that?

REGGIE

Quit stalling, I want some identification now.

CRUIKSHANK

I wouldn't lie on a license.

REGGIE

You can't prove it to me, can you? You're still trying to... Marriage license? Did you say marriage license?

CRUIKSHANK

Now don't change the subject. Just give me the stamps.

Reggie sits in his lap and wraps her arms around him. The scene shrinks to a small inset against black at the center of the frame. The inset is surrounded by other inset scenes throughout the movie showing Cruikshank's various aliases as she names them:

REGGIE

Oh, I love you, Adam, Alex, Peter, Brian, whatever your name is. Oh, I love you. I hope we have a lot of boys and we can name them all after you.

CRUIKSHANK

Well, before we start that, may I have the stamps?

She kisses him; he resists at first then gives in.

THE END

www.ingramcontent.com/pod-product-compliance
Lightning Source LLC
LaVergne TN
LVHW010615210626
841568LV00034B/488

* 9 7 9 8 3 5 0 5 0 2 2 5 1 *